Monsieur Pamplemousse on Probation

MICHAEL BOND was born in Newbury, Berkshire in 1926 and started writing whilst serving in the army during the Second World War. In 1958 the first book featuring his most famous creation, Paddington Bear, was published and many stories of his adventures followed. In 1983 he turned his hand to adult fiction and the detective cum gastronome par excellence Monsieur Pamplemousse was born.

Michael Bond was awarded the OBE in 1997 and in 2007 was made an Honorary Doctor of Letters by Reading University. He is married, with two grown-up children, and lives in London.

By Michael Bond

Monsieur Pamplemousse Afloat
Monsieur Pamplemousse on Probation
Monsieur Pamplemousse on Vacation
Monsieur Pamplemousse Hits the Headlines
Monsieur Pamplemousse and the Militant Midwives
Monsieur Pamplemousse and the French Solution
Monsieur Pamplemousse and the Carbon Footprint

Monsieur Pamplemousse on Probation

MICHAEL BOND

Allison & Busby Limited
12 Fitzroy Mews
London W1T 6DW
www.allisonandbusby.com

First published in Great Britain by Allison & Busby in 2000.
This paperback edition published by Allison & Busby in 2013.

A CIP catalogue record for this book is available from
the British Library.

10 9 8 7 6 5 4 3 2 1

ISBN 978-0-7490-1390-5

Typeset in 11/16 pt Century Schoolbook by
Allison & Busby Ltd.

The paper used for this Allison & Busby publication
has been produced from trees that have been legally sourced
from well-managed and credibly certified forests.

Printed and bound by
CPI Group (UK) Ltd, Croydon, CR0 4YY

CHAPTER ONE

Monsieur Henri Leclercq, Director of *Le Guide*, the oldest and most respected culinary bible in the whole of France, turned away from the window of his seventh-floor office as Monsieur Pamplemousse entered the room. Swivelling his chair in what was clearly a well-rehearsed movement, he came to rest in a position which ensured that his face was in deep shadow.

As he leant back and flicked an imaginary speck of dust from his dark blue pinstripe André Bardot tailored suit, a deep sigh filled the room. It was hard to tell if it was a hiss of escaping air emanating from within the luxurious folds of the black leather upholstery or whether it came from somewhere deep inside Monsieur Leclercq himself. It might even have been a mixture of the two, for it was a sound which exuded both opulence and long suffering.

He nodded towards a chair of rather less generous dimensions positioned in front of his desk. 'Please be seated, Pamplemousse.'

Another nod embraced a waiting figure at Monsieur Pamplemousse's side. 'Pommes Frites, too.'

Pommes Frites beat his master to it by a short head. After noisily slaking his thirst from a bowl of water someone, presumably Véronique, the Director's secretary, had put out for his benefit, he leapt up, settled himself down in a patch of sun, and closed his eyes. He knew the signs; they pointed to a long session of questions and answers. Monsieur Leclercq would be asking the questions, and with luck his master would be providing the answers. It was a good opportunity to catch up on lost sleep.

'*Excusez-moi, Monsieur*. The last few days have been very tiring for him.' Apologising for his companion's unseemly behaviour, Monsieur Pamplemousse gave Pommes Frites a nudge and pointed to the floor. '*Asseyez-vous*.'

Taking advantage of the momentary distraction, he stole a quick glance around the room, taking in as he did so other signs which, in his haste, Pommes Frites had failed to spot. The door to the drinks cabinet was firmly shut. Clearly, hospitality was not the order of the day, although he did note in passing an empty brandy glass on the Director's desk; a desk which although normally clear, was positively littered with the day's *journaux*. Not to put too fine a point on matters, it looked for all the world like a newsagent's kiosk at delivery time. He also noted that the right-hand lapel of Monsieur Leclercq's jacket bore the insignia of the *Légion d'honneur*, yet another pointer to the seriousness of the occasion.

Having changed places with his friend and mentor, Monsieur Pamplemousse shifted uneasily as he tried to make himself comfortable. In his haste, Pommes Frites had been less than meticulous in conserving his intake of water. But unlike the Director's executive chair, his own seat remained stationary. It had been set at a carefully calculated angle which ensured that the rays of the morning sun, deflected by the golden dome of the Hôtel des Invalides some four hundred metres away, those same rays that had so attracted Pommes Frites, landed fairly and squarely across his face. The signs were not auspicious.

The message summoning him to Headquarters had arrived at his home by special delivery late the previous evening. He had taken Doucette to the cinema, and the note had been in his mail box to greet him on their return. Short and to the point, it bade him report to the Director's office at nine o'clock sharp the following morning.

Interrupting Monsieur Pamplemousse's thoughts, the Director riffled through the pile of papers in front of him.

'I take it, Pamplemousse, you have seen the news.'

Monsieur Pamplemousse shook his head. 'No, *Monsieur*. I left early so that I could be here on time as you requested. The traffic in Montmartre is normally bad at this time of day . . .' He broke off, shielding his eyes as the Director held a copy of *Figaro* aloft. For a split second he could have sworn he saw a photograph of himself on the front page. A strangely distorted reproduction to be true, but the likeness was there nevertheless, as indeed was the location.

His heart sank as he was at last able to see the drift of the Director's line of questioning.

In recent weeks Monsieur Leclercq had been on one of his leadership kicks. It often happened when he returned from a business trip to the United States, where they were very keen on such things. His latest visit was no exception and *Le Guide* had since suffered accordingly. Memos couched in unfamiliar jargon appeared on the canteen notice board. Addressed TO ALL STAFF, they contained subheadings calculated to spread alarm and despondency around the building; phrases like 'Survival Courses', 'Maximising One's Potential', and the need to be 'Fully Stretched' were bandied about willy-nilly.

One by one staff had been plucked from their hiding places and dispatched to various parts of France, there to take part in assault courses the like of which they had only previously read about in books on the Gulf War. Rumour had it that there was even a photograph in circulation which showed Madame Grante, Head of the Accounts Department, wading through a salt marsh in the Camargue dressed in combat outfit and clutching a Kalashnikov assault rifle above her head, but since no one could lay claim to having actually seen a copy, it could have been one of Bernard's flights of fancy. Bernard was a dab hand at spreading rumours.

The sickness rate had risen to unprecedented heights. Applications for *bisques*, leave granted at a moment's notice without any reason having to be given (three days per annum max.), proliferated. And when those were used up, hitherto unmentioned relatives materialised out of the blue, only to drop dead within a matter of days.

Monsieur Pamplemousse, no stranger to the tricks of the trade, had managed to avoid his stint by one devious means or another, but in the end life finally caught up with him and from one of the remaining short straws he had drawn a week's survival course at a naval base in Boulogne.

There he had run foul of a fitness freak of the very worst kind, an ex-member of an elite undercover brigade who he was sure must retire to bed at night wearing a wetsuit and goggles rather than pyjamas. One way and another it had been a disastrous few days. Parts of him hadn't felt so stretched in years, and it had culminated in his being sent home early in disgrace.

Monsieur Leclercq rapped the offending item with the knuckles of his other hand before tossing it to one side.

'Explanations, Pamplemousse.'

Monsieur Pamplemousse decided to play for time. 'Shall I begin at the beginning, *Monsieur*?'

'If you must,' said the Director wearily.

'I simply suggest that in deference to your family motto,' said Monsieur Pamplemousse. '*Ab ovo usque ad mala*. From the beginning to the end.'

'I am well acquainted with the meaning of our family motto, Pamplemousse,' said the Director huffily. 'Please get on with it. I do not have all day.'

Monsieur Pamplemousse took a deep breath.

'It was very cold, *Monsieur*. Even colder than is usual for the time of year.'

'Survival courses, Pamplemousse,' said the Director sternly, 'take no account of climatic conditions. That is the whole point of them. The same qualities of leadership required for leading troops into battle in the Sahara desert during the

12

blazing heat of summer are equally necessary on a February day in Boulogne.'

Monsieur Pamplemousse decided he wasn't going down without a fight. 'With respect, *Monsieur*, I venture to suggest that leadership under fire is hardly one of the major qualities needed by an Inspector for *Le Guide*. A good sense of direction, yes. A knowledge of map-reading, the ability to work alone for long hours at a time, an analytical mind, taste buds honed to perfection, a good digestive system; all these things are necessary. But entries in *Le Guide* for both the Sahara desert and Boulogne are remarkably thin on the ground at any time of the year.'

The Director chose to ignore the interruption. Searching among the *journaux* he picked up a manila folder and opened it at a previously marked page.

'Your report makes unhappy reading, Pamplemousse. You not only failed to achieve the fifty per cent pass rate in any of the subjects covered by the course, in some areas you were actually given a minus mark, and Pommes Frites fared no better.

'*Par exemple*, it says here when your course instructor commanded you to jump into the harbour, instead of obeying orders you stood back and said "*Après vous.*"'

'That is true, *Monsieur*.'

'The poor man took you at your word and after swimming about fifty metres he looked over his shoulder and you were still standing on the quay. It is no wonder he was in a bad mood.'

'There was one basic problem, *Monsieur*.'

'Which was?'

'I cannot swim.'

'Why did you not tell him?'

'Swimming is his chosen profession, *Monsieur*. It is certainly not mine. Besides, he did not ask me.'

The Director clucked impatiently. 'That is a very negative attitude, Pamplemousse. Hardly what one might have expected from an ex-member of the Paris *Sûreté*, and certainly not up to the standards set by our illustrious founder.' Here Monsieur Leclercq paused to allow Monsieur Pamplemousse time in which to glance over his shoulder at a large oil painting hanging on the wall to his left.

As always, the subject's steely gaze provided no crumbs of comfort. Monsieur Pamplemousse sometimes wondered what pleasure, if any, Monsieur Hippolyte Duval had got out of life. As with *Michelin*, *Le Guide* had started off as a *vade mecum* for travellers, although unlike the former, and being first in the field by a small margin, it had been aimed at the cycling fraternity rather than those who were fortunate enough to own a motor car. Bernard always maintained Monsieur Duval looked

14

as though he suffered from chronic indigestion, but perhaps he had simply been permanently saddle sore.

'At the time, *Monsieur*, it seemed a very positive attitude. Boulogne harbour is not the most salubrious place at the best of times. People do not go there to "take" the water, but rather to throw things into it. It struck me that while awaiting the outgoing tide the harbour had managed to accumulate rather more than its fair share of the world's detritus, much of which one would hesitate to give a name to in polite society, especially since *les Anglaises* took to descending *en masse* in order to do their shopping in the local *supermarchés*.

'He then expected me to swim out to a vessel at anchor some twenty metres away, dive under it, and with luck emerge on the other side. In no way was I going to risk life and limb on what seemed to me to be an exceedingly hazardous, not to say pointless exercise. There were a number of perfectly good rowing boats to hand.'

'And what was Pommes Frites' excuse?' Despite his impatience at the direction the conversation was taking, Monsieur Leclercq's interest was obviously roused and he allowed himself a momentary digression. 'I see here he also refused to obey a twice-uttered command.'

'That happened when the Instructor, a man

15

of undoubted physical prowess but limited imagination, removed from Pommes Frites' mouth what he mistakenly assumed to be a lump of wood. He then threw it into the water so that it could be fetched. Doubtless, he was hoping to encourage both of us to dive in after it, but in the event we were not tempted. The object sank like a stone. I suspect that when Pommes Frites looked over the side of the jetty he reached much the same conclusion about the state of the water as I did.'

'And?'

'That was when he bit the Instructor, *Monsieur*. The "stick" happened to be a frozen *boudin noir*. He was warming it up in his mouth and not unnaturally took umbrage at seeing it thrown into the ocean instead of being served up in a bowl with some *pommes purée*, as he doubtless expected it would be.'

'Hmm.' The Director's eyes glazed over. 'This may sound a silly question, Pamplemousse, but may I ask what Pommes Frites was doing standing on a quayside in Boulogne in midwinter with a frozen *boudin noir* in his mouth?'

'I imagine he was looking for somewhere to bury it for safe keeping, *Monsieur*. After all, it was his birthday . . . but surrounded as he was by acres of concrete and cobblestones, suitable hiding places were few and far between.'

16

'Pommes Frites' birthday?' repeated the Director. 'Why was I not informed? It should be on file. Had I known I would have sent him a card.' Reaching out, he pressed a key and dictated a short note to his secretary.

Monsieur Pamplemousse acknowledged the compliment on behalf of his friend. 'I took the *boudin* with me to mark the occasion, *Monsieur*. It came from Coesnon in the rue Dauphine. They make them fresh every Tuesday and Thursday.'

'Aah!' In spite of himself, the Director gave a deep sigh. This time there was no mistaking the source. 'Coesnon. I know it well. Tell me, does Pommes Frites favour the chestnut flavoured variety or the ones with raisins?'

'He has Catholic tastes, *Monsieur*. As a special treat I bought him a selection. However, if pressed I would say he is particularly partial to the *boudin de campagne*. I noticed that after a cursory sniff he disposed of that one first and it is not in his nature to save the best until last; rather the reverse. He ate most of the others for breakfast; all except for one which he was saving for later and I have no idea which flavour that was. Now, we shall none of us ever know. I think if it ever surfaces it will be given a wide berth.'

'Saving his last *boudin* until later!' The Director gazed in awe at the recumbent figure lying next to Monsieur Pamplemousse, then he drew a line through an entry on a form in front of him. 'Would that we all had such strength of character, Pamplemousse,' he added meaningly. 'Such iron will to resist temptation when the occasion demands.

'Which brings me somewhat appositely,' he continued, 'to the matter in hand; the reason why I called you in at this hour of the day.' Once again the Director pointed to the pile of newspapers. 'Pamplemousse, the worst has happened. In the early hours of this morning I received a telephone call from an old friend, the head of one of our most respected press agencies, issuing a friendly warning.'

A small cloud momentarily blotted out the sun and Monsieur Pamplemousse caught another brief glimpse of his own likeness. 'The results of my exam are in the *journal*, *Monsieur*?'

The Director clucked impatiently. 'No, Pamplemousse, they are not, and let us pray they never will be. If your name is ever linked to that of *Le Guide* the ignominy will be hard to live down. No, worse than that, I fear. Far worse. I am referring to events which took place later that same day.'

Monsieur Pamplemousse stared at the picture. The black areas, which from a distance he had taken to be shadows, took on an ecclesiastical nature when seen at close quarters. Legs protruded at unseemly angles from a black gown. A face, looking straight up at the camera lens, was unmistakably his. Thank goodness he had unburdened himself to Doucette when he arrived home. It would have given her a terrible shock had she stumbled on it by accident.

'Pamplemousse! Are you listening?'

Monsieur Pamplemousse came to with a start as he realised he was being addressed.

'I repeat,' barked the Director, 'can you not be away from home for more than a day or two at a time without feeling the need to satisfy your carnal desires?'

'I assure you, *Monsieur*, it was not like that at all. Nothing could have been further from my mind. Pommes Frites and I had been out for a walk and we were taking a shortcut. As you may know, "lights out" in our billets was at twenty-two hundred hours and it seemed a good opportunity to practise our wall climbing. It is a very useful attribute when one is visiting strange restaurants, *Monsieur*. The element of surprise when arriving late at night can sometimes prove invaluable when preparing reports.'

'Spare me your sarcasm, Aristide,' said the Director. 'The pity is that you chose the wall of a convent on which to practise.'

'All walls look alike in the dark, *Monsieur*.'

'An unhappy choice of phrase in the circumstances,'

said the Director. 'The Mother Superior was convinced you were trying to rape her on the spot.'

'She happened to be doing her nightly patrol,' said Monsieur Pamplemousse. 'Unfortunately I landed on top of her as she was going past.'

'That,' said the Director sternly as he retrieved his copy of *Figaro*, 'is patently obvious from this photograph. It is the stuff of which headlines are made. And Pommes Frites? What is he doing, glowering lasciviously over the unfortunate victim when he should have been going to her rescue?'

'That is not a glower, *Monsieur*. That is his concerned expression.'

'The article maintains that he was attacking her.'

'It only goes to show people shouldn't believe all they read in the *journaux*,' said Monsieur Pamplemousse.

'But people do, Aristide. That is the trouble . . . people do. It is my belief that the media has it within its power to bring about the destruction of mankind if it ever feels so disposed.'

'He was merely trying to lick her better, *Monsieur*,' said Monsieur Pamplemousse lamely. '*Chiens*' saliva is believed to be rich in healing qualities. He was as concerned as I was at the turn of events.'

'Not a story that would stand up in court, Pamplemousse, I fear,' said the Director soberly.

'Parallels might be drawn between yourself and a poster advertising Bela Lugosi playing the part of Dracula. The fact that you made good your escape before the police arrived will undoubtedly go against you.'

'Escape?' Monsieur Pamplemousse looked suitably offended. 'By then it was five minutes to lights out, *Monsieur*. Discipline is very strict at the naval base and I had no wish to be locked out. Having tendered our sincere apologies to the good lady and made sure she was none the worse for the experience . . . no broken bones . . . no torn ligaments . . . we shook hands. She even thanked me for my courteous behaviour and rewarded Pommes Frites with a pat on the head.'

'That is not what she is saying now.'

'With respect, *Monsieur*, people often see things differently in the cold light of day. That is why in France when two cars are involved in a collision an accident report must be filled in by both parties on the spot. In that way neither side can change their story at a later date.'

'Perhaps you should have filled in a collision report yourself,' said the Director dryly.

'The facts will speak for themselves, *Monsieur* . . .'

'Facts, as you well know, Pamplemousse, can be distorted beyond measure in a court of law. Besides, it is all there, the whole sordid incident. Recorded for posterity on infrared film. The Mother Superior entering shot innocently going about her nightly duties without a care in the world. Her worry beads an unnecessary adjunct to her peace of mind. The next moment, there she is, lying on the path with her assailant spreadeagled on top of her.'

'Infrared film?' repeated Monsieur Pamplemousse. 'In a seminary?' It was no wonder the photograph in *Figaro* had a strange, almost surreal quality to it.

'The nun in charge of security happens to be an ex-lawyer who has taken the vow,' said the Director. 'In her time she specialised in prosecutions involving crimes committed against other members of her sex. Fellow man is not a phrase that springs happily to her lips. That is why I fear the worst. She will leave no stone unturned until she brings you to book. It needs but one of your ex-colleagues to point their finger, or *Paris Match* to scent a possible scandal and send one of their ace reporters. I shudder to think what will happen if word reaches Rome. Sales of our Italian edition will plummet.

'But you know as well as I do what the press are like once they get the bit between their teeth. Fortunately, the friend who alerted me managed to kill the story before it went too far. So far only one *journal* has picked it up, but it is only a matter of time. Some young blood anxious to prove himself must have dug up an old photograph taken at the time of your unfortunate affair with the chorus girls at the *Folies* and put two and two together, only this time it will be much worse. There are those who would argue that mathematically speaking one Mother Superior is equal to, or greater than, a whole line of chorus girls. I can see the headlines now: "Pamplemousse Strikes Again."'

'A good lawyer would tear it to pieces, *Monsieur* . . .'

'Good lawyers cost money, Aristide. Besides, where there is smoke more often than not there is fire and mud sticks.'

Faced with such a barrage of unarguable aphorisms Monsieur Pamplemousse hesitated.

'What do you suggest, *Monsieur*?' he asked meekly.

'There is only one course open to us,' said Monsieur Leclercq. 'You must lie low for a while. It will blow over. These things always do. My informant has seen to that. To use a technical expression, the story has been spiked for the time being, and so far neither *Figaro* nor any of the other *journaux* have made the connection with *Le Guide*. We must ensure it stays that way.

'*Alors!*' The Director raised his hands to high heaven before consulting the folder once again. 'I have been reading your annual medical report. The word "stress" is mentioned several times. We have perhaps been overworking you of late. One forgets you are no longer as young as you were. We none of us are. Perhaps you should have a thorough check-up.'

'Madame Pamplemousse would not be happy, *Monsieur*. She takes the view that if things are working they are best left alone.'

'Nonsense, Pamplemousse,' said the Director severely. 'I'm sure you take your car in for a regular service. Why should you balk at the thought of taking your own body in for a check-up simply because the doctor might find something wrong with it?'

'Had I gone into the sea at Boulogne as instructed,' broke in Monsieur Pamplemousse, 'I may have needed a post-mortem. As *Monsieur* may well discover when it is his turn,' he added meaningly.

The Director brushed aside the interruption with what might have been construed by some as unseemly haste.

'I gave the matter considerable thought on my way into the office this morning, Aristide,' he began, 'and it seems to me that this unhappy affair could be an opportunity to kill several *oiseaux* with one stone. Clearly both you and Pommes Frites need to keep a low profile for the time being. At least until all the fuss has died down. Equally clearly a rest would not come amiss for both of you.'

As if to underline what the Director was saying, Pommes Frites gave vent to a loud snore at that point.

'He is still recovering from his birthday celebrations,' explained Monsieur Pamplemousse. 'We spent the evening in a local waterside bistro and one thing led to another . . .'

'Please,' Monsieur Leclercq held up his hand, 'spare me the sordid details, Pamplemousse. It simply goes to prove my point. A change of scene will do you both the world of good. A breath of fresh country air . . . a chance to recharge your respective batteries.

'One might almost say, Aristide,' he continued casually, and had Monsieur Pamplemousse not momentarily lowered his guard while he allowed his mind to dwell on other matters, it might have struck him as being perhaps a little too casual, '. . . one might almost say that a spell close to your roots might work wonders. It will give you a chance to take stock as it were. In short, what I have in mind is a week in the Auvergne.'

Monsieur Leclercq paused to let his announcement sink in, and while doing so gazed affectionately at the portrait on the wall, almost as though he were about to genuflect, but in the end he thought better of it.

'Strangely enough,' continued the Director, 'it was to the Auvergne that I was sent by our founder shortly after I joined *Le Guide*. I haven't been back since. It was before I was married and I suspect

Chantal would find it a little too rugged for her tastes. Queuing for a shower at the end of a long corridor in the morning along with half a dozen hardy individuals with hairy legs is not exactly her idea of fun; she prefers her creature comforts. But I remember it well. I felt the whole thing was a kind of test and I very nearly blotted my copybook.

'It was early autumn and the *patron* of the very first hostelry I stayed at served the most delicious *pommes aligot*. It was made with very young *cantal* cheese.

'And *crème fraiche* of course.' Monsieur Pamplemousse was unable to resist breaking in.

'Of course. But you must remember it was the first time I had ever tasted it and it was an eye-opener. As an accompaniment to a simple *crépinette* of pig's liver and mixed vegetables fresh from the garden, the whole wrapped in lacy caul fat and cooked in the oven, it was nothing short of sensational.

'I had begun the meal with tiny local sausages wrapped in pastry, and afterwards I was given the most delicious pie made with pears and walnuts.

'On the strength of what I must admit in hindsight was a somewhat flowery report, a number of readers drove all the way down from Paris to dine there, but he was a curmudgeonly old character and often he wouldn't let them in. Those who did manage to get a table couldn't understand a word he was saying.

There were numerous complaints and for a while my career was in jeopardy. It taught me a valuable lesson though, and Monsieur Duval had the good sense to see it that way.'

Monsieur Pamplemousse could picture it all. He had come across such people before, especially in the remoter parts of the Auvergne. Individualists who behaved as though they had a grudge against society. You wondered how on earth they had ever become involved in running a hotel. And yet, unable to read or write, they often cooked like a dream.

'I can still recall the hills with cattle grazing in fields of yellow gentian,' mused the Director. 'Peat bogs with their tiny herbaceous willow trees in the valleys. The surprise at suddenly coming across vast areas of extinct volcanoes, and the mountains with their fields awash with wild flowers. The occasional *buron*, those stone huts shepherds used to take shelter in. And everywhere you went, hams hanging from the joists and fresh water bubbling up out of the ground. But most of all I remember the fresh, clean air of the mountains.'

Monsieur Pamplemousse shifted in his chair as Monsieur Leclercq began to wax lyrical. He felt tempted to say that they were the only things about the Auvergne which were memorable, but he knew better than to interrupt Monsieur Leclercq when he had the bit between his teeth.

'I remember, too, the wild salmon from the Allier,' continued the Director. 'Do you realise, Aristide, that some two years after they are born they swim downriver to the sea and travel as far afield as Greenland, there to feed on the shrimps which give them their colour, before swimming all the way back to the place of their birth. Perhaps, Aristide, although your own marine activities hardly qualify to be mentioned in the same breath, you, too, should return to the place of your birth.'

Monsieur Pamplemousse could contain himself no longer. 'All you say may be true of the Auvergne in the late spring and summer, *Monsieur*,' he said. 'But the summers are short-lived and we are talking about the depths of winter. In winter it is worse than Boulogne.'

'There you go again, Pamplemousse,' snorted the Director. 'This negative attitude of yours is becoming a habit. It ill becomes you . . .'

'But, *Monsieur*, the climate is harsh. Roads are often impassable from December to May. There is ice on the *inside* of the windows. People have been known to die of the cold. There is a very good reason why half the bistros in Paris are owned by men from the Auvergne. They escaped from it all as soon as they were old enough.'

'Pamplemousse.' The Director gathered the papers on his desk into a neat pile. 'It is an order. I have booked you in at Dulac under *Le Guide*'s newly instituted code name of the week – Monsieur Blanc.'

'Dulac!' Mention of the Auvergne's only three Stock Pot hotel stopped Monsieur Pamplemousse dead in his tracks. Owing to *Le Guide*'s policy of never using their Inspectors on home territory for fear they might be recognised, it had never occurred to him that he might be given the chance of a visit. It was a signal, perhaps never to be repeated, honour, and certainly not one to be turned down in a hurry.

'It is open in February?' Pouligny was only a matter of twenty or so kilometres from where he had been born. It was the nearest village of any size and in his day it had boasted two hotels. But like most establishments in the region their opening and closing times during the winter months had been variable to say the least.

'All through the year. It is the only hotel in France for which Michelin have seen fit to create a special symbol of a snowplough rampant. They have a fleet of them standing by ready for any emergency. Subject to your findings, Pamplemousse, I suggest we follow suit in next year's *Guide*.'

Monsieur Pamplemousse felt a surge of excitement. Despite his earlier misgivings, taste buds began to show signs of life. André Dulac's was a rare, a God-given talent. His rise to fame had been nothing short of meteoric. Taking over the hotel from his father and starting off with a mere Bar Stool – the symbol indicating it was worth stopping off for lunch if you happened to be in the area, he had gone on to win his first Stock Pot a year later. Following that with an additional Stock Pot every two years, until he reached the maximum of three was unheard of.

The Director allowed himself a smile. 'I thought that might cause you to change your tune, Aristide. A different kettle of *poisson, n'est-ce pas?*'

'I have yet to visit it myself. That is a pleasure yet to come. But in the meantime, in the most discreet possible way you could perhaps combine business with pleasure. The time is coming up when we must finalise the entries for this year's *Guide*. As I'm sure you know, our computer has just completed its analysis of all the year's reports, a mammoth task, and its printout shows that Dulac is in line for this year's top award, the Golden Stock Pot Lid. It is a toss-up between Dulac and Ducasse, with the odds, the merest fraction of a decimal point, in favour of Dulac. Not even Ducasse can be in two places at once, and since he donned Robuchon's mantle in Paris as well as still keeping a watchful eye on the stoves at Monte Carlo doubts have been raised.

'But in the past few weeks strange reports have been coming through regarding Dulac. First there was the unfortunate business of the recycled lettuce leaf. You heard about that, of course?'

Monsieur Pamplemousse nodded. He'd been in the North at the time, but news had spread like wildfire. Guilot, an acknowledged expert on all things to do with salad ingredients, had been paying a routine visit. Ordering a simple *salade verte* to accompany his *filets de veau au citron* he was prepared to swear that, far from being freshly prepared, one of the leaves was sodden and had clearly been recycled from a previous serving.

'It can happen, *Monsieur*.'

'Not in a three Stock Pot establishment, Pamplemousse. Especially not in a three Stock Pot establishment in line for our supreme accolade of a *Chapeau d'Or*.'

Monsieur Pamplemousse took the implied reproof in good part. The Director was right, of course. Standards must never be allowed to slip; not for a second, otherwise they were all wasting their time. It made a mockery of the whole thing.

Reputations built up over the years could be destroyed in a moment.

'Now, there is Loudier.'

'How is he, *Monsieur*?'

'He has been offered counselling, but so far he has refused it.'

It was a cruel twist of fate. It was poor old

Loudier, the *doyen* of the Inspectors and now nearing retirement, who had been largely responsible for putting Monsieur Dulac's name forward for the award of his first Stock Pot. In those days the hotel had been known simply as the Hôtel Moderne. Then Dulac had called it after his grandfather, Prosper Dulac. It wasn't until the award of the third Stock Pot that it had become plain Dulac and by that time he was already in grand new premises just outside the village.

After the affair of the lettuce leaf it was Loudier who had been sent to give the establishment a final pre-publication check. It had been largely meant as a treat on the Director's part, but he had returned in haste to recount a particularly nasty experience with a worm.

'Is it true he found it in his *salade parmentière, Monsieur*?'

'Worse, Pamplemousse. It was half a *lumbricidae.* A large one, clearly fresh from the *jardin.*'

'Which end, *Monsieur*?'

'The end is immaterial, Pamplemousse. A worm is a worm. Not wishing to reveal his identity, Loudier managed to contain himself until he was outside where he deposited it whence it came from. The mark of a true professional.'

'You mentioned killing several birds with one stone, *Monsieur*,' said Monsieur Pamplemousse, quickly changing the subject. 'Do I take it there is another *oiseau* to be slain?'

'Ah, yes, Aristide.' The Director made play of pretending he had forgotten. 'Thank you for reminding me. Rather than drive down in your *deux chevaux*, which may well be under scrutiny by the media, I wonder if you could possibly do an old friend of mine a small favour?

'It is a matter of finding someone reliable to deliver what is known as a "Twingo" to an address in Roanne. I'm sure you know the model. They are currently all the rage; much in demand by the "in" set. Every other car parked outside the boutiques in the avenue Montaigne seems to be one.'

Monsieur Pamplemousse hesitated. 'And after I have delivered it, *Monsieur*? It is still another fifty kilometres or so to Pouligny.'

The Director brushed the problem aside. 'You can either hire a car to complete the journey or else use a taxi. Either way, at the end of your stay you and Pommes Frites can return to Paris by train.'

'When would you like me to leave, *Monsieur*?'

Monsieur Leclercq glanced down at his watch. 'Now seems as good a time as any, Pamplemousse.'

'Now?' Monsieur Pamplemousse sat bolt upright. 'But I haven't even unpacked from my last trip.'

'So much the better,' said the Director unfeelingly. 'Procrastination is the thief of time. The sooner you set off the better. I suggest tomorrow morning at the very latest.'

Monsieur Pamplemousse considered the matter for a moment or two. He was aware of how fortunate he was. On the other hand everything was happening much too quickly for his liking. When he'd arrived at the office that morning, he hadn't known quite what to expect. What he certainly hadn't bargained for was going off on his travels again quite so soon. Doucette would not be pleased.

From somewhere he heard a disembodied voice saying, 'Of course, *Monsieur*.'

The Director looked relieved as he rose from his chair. Clearly the whole thing had been preying on his mind.

'I would prefer it if you didn't mention this to anyone, Aristide. It might be misconstrued in some quarters.'

'Of course, *Monsieur*.'

'Good.' Monsieur Leclercq removed a piece of white pasteboard from his wallet and made the journey round his desk in record time. 'Here is the address where the car is to be collected. I will ensure that it is ready first thing tomorrow morning along with the rest of your instructions.

'Enjoy your drive. As for Dulac, I shall await your report with interest. *Bonne chance*.'

'What shall I tell the others, *Monsieur*?'

34

Monsieur Leclercq looked at him in some surprise. 'Simply say you are on probation, Pamplemousse. Once word gets around the office about the goings on in Boulogne it will sound more than likely.'

Monsieur Pamplemousse knew from experience that the Director was a past master in the art of bringing an interview to an end, but even so it had to be something of a record.

He wasn't even given the chance to say goodbye to Véronique. Before he had time to open his mouth, Monsieur Leclercq's telephone rang, almost as though it were prearranged, and the farewell handshake was converted through the open doorway into a gesture denoting he required his secretary's services. Véronique raised one eyebrow in mute apology as she swept past clutching her notebook.

Even Pommes Frites, normally alert to his master's comings and goings, only just made it through the door before it closed firmly behind him.

Monsieur Pamplemousse shrugged as he let himself out into the corridor.

How did the old saying go? 'When one door shuts another opens.' Part of the fun in life was not knowing where the next one would lead to.

CHAPTER TWO

Monsieur Pamplemousse dialled 01 49 36 10 10 for *Les Taxis Bleus* and waited a moment or two until a girl's voice cut in over the synthesised music. He gave his telephone number, waited for her to come back confirming his address, then relaxed to the strains of music again.

'*Un* Mercedes *gris*. Six minutes.' Almost at once the girl's voice broke in again, terminating their brief encounter with a click as she transferred her attention to the next customer in the queue. Having been lulled into a state of unreadiness, Monsieur Pamplemousse leapt into action. It was typical of life. Eight o'clock on a wet morning in Paris, when you would expect there to be delays, and what happened? You were left with six minutes to say your goodbyes, grab your belongings and race down as many flights of stairs. At that time of day there was no point in waiting for the antiquated lift.

With Pommes Frites hot on his heels, he made it down to the street in a fraction over five minutes, his cheeks barely dry from Doucette's farewell kiss.

The Place Marcel Aymé was deserted. There were no men lurking in doorways, cameras at the ready. Equally, there was no *Taxi Bleu*.

Monsieur Pamplemousse took shelter in the doorway while he got his breath back, leaving Pommes Frites to brave the drizzle as he made his way to the nearest lamp post. Exactly two minutes later there was a swish of water on wet cobblestones and a grey Mercedes pulled up at the kerb.

Seeing Monsieur Pamplemousse's luggage the driver climbed out of the car, turned his jacket collar up, and with a certain amount of ill grace went round to the boot.

Monsieur Pamplemousse made great play of looking at his watch. 'The traffic is bad today?' he suggested as he made his way to the kerb. His joke fell as flat as the leaden sky above.

The man gave a grunt as he slammed the lid shut. 'It is the hour of *affluence*.'

Clearly he was in no mood for pleasantries. Monsieur Pamplemousse handed over the card the Director had given him, then opened the rear door and stood waiting.

'He is coming too?' Catching sight of the driver staring at him, Pommes Frites pointedly shook himself dry before climbing into the back and making himself comfortable on the rear seat.

'You have an objection?'

The driver glanced up at the rear-view mirror, decided against whatever it was he'd been about to say, and pressed a button on his meter instead. The standing charge went up. There was a price to pay for everything, especially wet bloodhounds making their presence felt.

Having executed a U-turn, they drove in silence back down the hill from Montmartre. Monsieur Pamplemousse wasn't too sorry. He had other things on his mind and Pommes Frites looked equally happy to be left to his own devices as he attended to his ablutions.

After waiting for the lights at the bottom, they headed east along the rue Clignancourt, eventually meeting up with the boulevard Barbès, where they joined the stream of traffic heading south.

There was something odd about the whole thing. Normally, the details, the booking of a taxi and the arrangements for picking up the new car, would have been left to Véronique, but he had a feeling she knew nothing about it. She certainly hadn't mentioned it when he'd arrived at the office the previous morning. It had been all commiserations about his trip to Boulogne: a case of 'there, but for the grace of the good Lord, go the rest of us, as we probably will in the fullness of time.' The Director must have taken care of the whole thing himself.

He'd phoned through later in the day. 'Make sure you reach Roanne soon after two o'clock, Pamplemousse' had been his parting shot. 'And don't worry about filling in a P49. Let me know how much it all comes to and we'll work it out when you get back.' It could only mean he must be wanting to keep it from Madame Grante as well.

Doucette had been characteristically blunt about it. 'You mark my words. He's up to something. It doesn't add up. He must have known about the car for some while. The business about your going into hiding only came up yesterday. It's like Jules always says: "Nine times out of ten when people enquire the price of a house on behalf of a friend, it's for themselves but they don't want to let on."' Doucette's brother was an estate agent.

The rain, which had seemed set for the day, began to ease as they crossed the Seine via the Pont Notre Dame; umbrellas were still up, the *gendarmes* standing guard outside the Préfecture de Police sheltered inside their plastic sentry boxes, but by the time they reached the fringes of the fourteenth *arrondissement* it had stopped altogether.

Dividing his time between negotiating the traffic

in the Place Denfert-Rochereau and studying a pocket street guide spread out across his steering wheel, the driver paused for a moment to exchange unpleasantries with the driver of an articulated *camion*, then he pointed up at the sky. A tiny shaft of sunshine had broken through a gap in the clouds.

The whole episode having clearly put him in a better mood he slowed down to a more leisurely pace, made a right turn, then a left followed by another right, and moments later pulled up alongside a row of anonymous buildings, mostly shuttered to the outside world.

'Is this it?' Monsieur Pamplemousse looked in vain for the familiar black on yellow insignia of a Renault agency. All he saw was a yellow Twingo parked on the pavement outside a nondescript building which could have housed practically anything.

'It is the address you gave me, *Monsieur*.'

Monsieur Pamplemousse read the inscription on the card as the driver handed it back to him. He hadn't given it more than a passing glance before, now he wished he had. Years in the Paris *Sûreté* had taught him to be wary of anyone calling themselves an Import-Export agency. In his experience the words were suspect in any language.

Paying off the taxi he collected his baggage and approached the Twingo. The door on the driver's side was locked. Ever curious, Pommes Frites joined him, rested his paws on the bonnet, then nearly jumped out of his skin as a metallic voice barked out: 'STAND CLEAR. SYSTEM ARMED.'

The sound brought a man wearing a white coat hurrying out of a side door. He was carrying a clipboard.

'Monsieur Pamplemousse?'

'*Oui.*'

Pointedly examining the bonnet to make sure there were no scratches, the man took a key fob from his pocket, used a small attachment to trigger off a second announcement: 'SYSTEM DISARMED', then pointed a key in the direction of the inside rear-view mirror. There was an immediate click from both doors.

'I normally drive a Citroën 2CV,' said Monsieur Pamplemousse defensively. 'One of the earlier models.'

'Ah!' said the man, as though that said it all.

Handing over the keys, he detached an A5 manila envelope from the clipboard. Beneath it there was a delivery note ready for signing, and with that simple formality completed he bid them both *bonne journée*, turned on his heels and left them to it.

It was all a bit disappointing. Gone were the days when you received the equivalent of a cockpit check before you were allowed anywhere near the driving seat of a new car, let alone touch the controls.

The engine started at the first turn of the key. As he eased the car off the pavement and onto the road Monsieur Pamplemousse wondered what the man normally dealt in. Whatever it was, it certainly wasn't cars. He couldn't help wondering what was so special about buying a Twingo in Paris when they must be readily available at dealers all over France.

Not wishing to be seen opening his instructions, he drove off straight away, adjusting the electric wing mirrors and familiarising himself with the ergonomics of the dashboard as he went. It was simplicity itself. A digital display in the central console showed his speed in figures large enough for the driver in the car behind him to read. All the other information he might need: time, total and trip mileage, was his at the touch of a button on the end of the windscreen and rearscreen wash/wipe stalk.

He turned a knob in front of him and warm air filtered into the compartment. The ventilation fan control to its right increased the flow. Such niceties normally took a good fifteen minutes to bring about in his *deux chevaux*.

Retracing the route the taxi driver had taken, Monsieur Pamplemousse circumnavigated the Place Denfert-Rochereau, then headed towards the *périphérique*. Firmly ensconced alongside him Pommes Frites occupied himself by eyeing the passers-by with a lordly air, only transferring his attention to the occupants of other cars when they joined the A6 autoroute.

His new-found sense of pride and importance lasted until they were some forty kilometres or so outside Paris and his master stopped to take a ticket from a machine at the Péage de Fleury. At that point he decided he might try the back seat for a change. He sensed a long drive ahead.

All the same, had Pommes Frites been employed as the canine motoring correspondent of one of the better daily *journaux*, he would have awarded his master's new car full marks in practically every respect. Apart from the initial shock when it had spoken to him in what he considered was an unnecessarily harsh, not to say unfriendly voice, it was comfortable, draught-free and undeniably quiet. It was also surprisingly roomy. If he had a complaint it had to do with there being no canvas top; a fact which he had discovered soon after they reached the autoroute and he tried to poke his head out through the roof in order to get a bit of fresh air. But then, you couldn't have everything.

As the barrier went up and Monsieur Pamplemousse set off in earnest he tried out the radio. The morning's weather forecast had not been good. Snow was falling in the mountains of central France. Glancing up he saw the information panel on the overheard gantry showed 09.17 and confirmed the falling temperature. At least when those two staples, time and weather, were shown it meant there were no hazards in the immediate vicinity.

Searching for a news bulletin so that he could bring himself up to date, he came across a station playing a Joe Pass record – an old Django Reinhardt number – 'Douce Ambience'. The hi-fi stereo with its four different sound sources made his own radio with a single loudspeaker below the dashboard sound tinny.

Monsieur Pamplemousse suddenly felt better as the combination of guitar, bass and drums set his fingers and his left foot tapping. It seemed a fitting accompaniment to the journey; underscoring the return to his childhood so to speak. He'd grown up with the music of the Quintet of the Hot Club of France, and the music you grew up with stayed with you for the rest of your life, dating you as surely as any birth certificate. It was a sadness that he'd never had the chance to share his pleasure with Doucette. In 1953, at the ridiculously early age of forty-three, Reinhardt had died of a stroke. They had missed seeing Joe Pass when he was playing in Paris, and now he, too, had departed this world. You should always seize hold of opportunities when they came your way. Which, of course, was exactly what he was doing driving south on the A6.

Helping himself to a sweet from a small bag in the side pocket of the door (it was the same colour as the paintwork, yellow, another thoughtful touch of Twingo chicness) he moved the envelope lying on top of the dashboard to avoid its reflection on the windscreen.

What Doucette didn't understand was that the Director enjoyed playing his cards close to his chest. That was the way he was and he would never change.

What was the other thing he'd said on the phone? 'Everything will be down in writing. Make sure you study it carefully before committing it to memory and destroying it.' His voice had sounded slightly muffled, as though he'd had his hand over the mouthpiece. Since he'd been phoning from home, it must mean it was something he didn't want his wife, Chantal, to know about.

Monsieur Pamplemousse gave it another twenty minutes or so and then couldn't contain himself any longer.

Exiting the autoroute at the Aire de Villiers, he parked under some trees near the children's play area, and reached for the envelope. Aside from two small children looking for all the world like miniature space-persons in their moon boots and padded anoraks, the place was empty. Pommes Frites eyed them through the window and decided against joining in; the weather was clouding over again and he'd only just dried out.

Slitting open the carefully sealed envelope, Monsieur Pamplemousse removed a grey wallet containing all the usual paraphernalia; handbook, service manual, a 227-page list of agents worldwide (not surprisingly, the address where he'd taken delivery of the car didn't get a mention), details of the Philips RC388 Car System (radio was obviously a dirty word) and a leaflet congratulating him on purchasing a fine security alarm system. They could say that again.

Tucked away inside a pocket was a smaller sealed manila envelope bearing his name. Slitting it open, he found a sheet of plain, unheaded white typing paper inside.

'Dear Aristide,' he read. 'Please treat this car as you would your own. Make sure Pommes Frites wipes his paws thoroughly before entering.'

'Now he tells me!' thought Monsieur Pamplemousse. 'He'll be wanting me to gift wrap it next.'

He read on and as he did so any thoughts he might have had about taking a leisurely stroll around the rest area before he began the journey proper, perhaps viewing the bronze statues dotted about amongst the Mediterranean Pines, or lingering over the displays of soil from the Forest of Fontainbleau, disappeared from his mind.

The Director's note wasn't at all what he had expected. He read through it again, committed the whole thing to memory as instructed, then tore the note into small pieces and deposited the remains in a nearby rubbish bin before setting off.

Glancing up at the rear-view mirror, Monsieur Pamplemousse made sure Pommes Frites was safely settled, then put his foot down and accelerated out into the slow lane between two large southbound *camions*. Out of respect for someone else's new car he stayed where he was for a while before pulling out into the middle lane where he settled down to a steady 90kph. He had no wish to spend the journey stuck between lorries in the slow lane; on the other hand, neither did he want to be caught in the fast lane doing less than the statutory 80kph minimum. He checked the time with his Cupillard Rième wristwatch. All being well, he should be in Roanne just after 14.00 as instructed.

And in Roanne it would be goodbye Twingo. Without feeling in any way disloyal, he had to admit to rather more than a passing pang of regret. When his old car finally reached retirement age the present one would be high on his list of possible replacements. Pommes Frites clearly approved of it. He was fast asleep again, a look of bliss on his face. One could wish for no better recommendation.

The message from the Director was precise and,

as was his wont, couched in terms he might well have used had he been addressing a congenital idiot: 'Leave the car in the parking area in the Place des Promenades Populle near the *gare*. If you can find a suitable space where the rear end is facing a brick wall, so much the better. I suggest you try and find a spot near to where I am told there is the statue erected to the poor. Make sure the engine is immobilised, the doors are locked, and that you are not overlooked, then leave the keys in the exhaust pipe, making sure they are out of sight. Above all, remember, *anonymat* must be maintained at all costs.'

Given that the note was written in Monsieur Leclercq's own hand, he could have said it all in his office, or even over the phone the night before. Perhaps Doucette was right. It bore all the hallmarks of hasty planning. He wondered what would have happened had he still been in Boulogne. And why so much cloak and dagger stuff about the simple act of delivering a new car?

Monsieur Pamplemousse tried to shrug the whole thing off, but he was conscious of a growing sense of unease the further south he went.

Perhaps it was the thought of going back to the scene of his childhood; something he'd always avoided doing. Life had been hard when he was a boy and part of him had no wish to return. It was

49

no wonder mass emigration to Paris had helped the capital earn its reputation for being the Auvergne's largest city.

That apart, there had been the war. It was impossible to explain to anyone who hadn't experienced it what it had been like; it had brought out the best and the worst in people, but after a fashion life had gone on. Most people had no wish to be heroes or to try and change the course of history. They were content to let things take their course, and who could blame them?

Another thing about the present situation. It was *Le Guide*'s policy not to have their Inspectors report on establishments too close to their home territory in case they were recognised. Not many people connected his present job with the years he had spent in the *Sûreté*, but there was always the risk. The last time he had been within a hundred kilometres of the area was when he'd spend a few days in Vichy with the American, Mrs Van Dorman. That, too, had been at the behest of the Director and look how it had ended up. She'd been lucky to escape the electric chair.

Not that many people would remember him, of course. He'd been away too long.

Soon after entering the Soanne Valley, Mâcon came into view, the flat pink-tiled roofs of the houses marking the transition between north and south.

Then a series of *panneaux marrons* in between trees thick with mistletoe, displayed signs welcoming visitors to Beaujolais, its *monts* and its *vignobles*, and his mood began to oscillate again as memories of happier times came flooding back.

There had been good things, too. Nature compensated for its shortcomings in other directions. Spring was always late arriving, but when it did there were wild daffodils in profusion, snowdrops, celandines and cowslips, and they had multiplied still further since it had become against the law to pick them. Violets flowered alongside lingering pockets of snow heralding the bounties to come; fungi of all kinds, and the first of the *fraises du bois*.

Then summer would arrive with a rush and there would be blue scabious in amongst the cow parsley. There was wildlife galore: marmot, mountain sheep, deer, boar roaming free, and cattle everywhere. Food was basic, but it was plentiful. The Director was right; it had a lot to offer.

Coming off the Autoroute de Soleil just before the main Péage de Villefranche, he drove out of town on the D38 and, following the signs for Roanne, passed a turning for the Route de Beaujolais.

Beaujolais! He'd been practically weaned on it, but in his day it had been quaffed out of pots drawn from the cask, not racked and re-racked within an inch of its life so that it could be bottled and despatched at speed to the four corners of the world in order that people could pronounce on what was left of its virtues.

Later in the year the same sign would be the signal for the more intrepid to seek out the little village of Vaux-en-Beaujolais, setting for Chevallier's bestselling political satire, *Clochemerle*. Over the years its *pissoir* had become famous; a shrine to the power of marketing *Beaujolais Nouveau*. He told himself not to be grumpy. If that was what gave people pleasure and made others prosper, then so be it. At least there were signs of a renaissance; *vignerons* who were working hard to raise the level again.

Once clear of Villefranche, the road began to climb steadily, heading towards the foothills of the Auvergne. On large-scale maps it showed up as a vast area of nothingness; *la France profonde*, the unexplored region. A day's travel away from home had always been an adventure into the unknown.

The smaller-scale maps contained within the pages of *Le Guide* revealed for the most part a gastronomic wilderness without so much as a single Bar Stool, *Le Guide*'s symbol for somewhere to stop for lunch. The fact that it was surrounded on all sides by restaurants of note – Roanne, where he was heading, had Troisgros; Collonges-au-Mont-d'Or outside Lyon had Bocuse; and the Rhône Valley to the east, full of riches – only served to emphasise the dearth of good restaurants.

Now that Pierre Gagnaire in St Étienne had gone, closed down and moved to Paris, like so many before him, the one shining light, the single beacon shining in the wilderness, was Dulac, and by the sound of it even he was having his troubles.

Monsieur Pamplemousse was so busy with his thoughts he very nearly collided with another car at a lethal road junction just after Les Olmes, where the D38 joined the N7. Gesticulations were exchanged. The Director wouldn't have been pleased. To say that it was all changed since he was last there would have gone down like a lead balloon.

Another 60km. Say, three quarters of an hour. He checked the time again. The clock said 13.30. He would be just about right.

After St Symphorien he hit the main road into the city and fast traffic started to build up as if from nowhere. As always, everyone else was in a tearing hurry and seemed to know exactly where they were going. Working on the theory that since Roanne's most famous restaurant was right opposite the *gare*, and as with most three Stock Pot establishments probably even better signposted than anything else in the town, and since the Director had told him the Place des Promenades Populle was right by the railroad station, he couldn't go far wrong if he aimed for Troisgros.

His theory worked. Ten minutes later and he was circumnavigating a large tree-lined park, the perimeter of which was lined with cars. The Director's instruction to seek out a parking bay near a wall suddenly seemed optimistic. It looked as though he would be lucky to find anywhere at all to park. Moreover, there didn't seem much in the way of activity, just a few odd cars crawling round the inner road, those at the wheel looking in much the same pessimistic state of mind as he was.

Checking the nearest pay and display machine, the Director's reasoning that he should arrive soon after 14.00 became clear. The list of charges showed that parking was free between the hours of 12.00 and 14.00. Before and after that it rose from a minimum of 1Fr every fifteen minutes to a maximum of 10Fr for nine hours. Clearly most people either overstayed their lunch time and risked a fine, or they paid their full whack at the start of the day.

Monsieur Pamplemousse's heart sank. There had been no mention in the Director's note about what to do in the event that he couldn't find anywhere to leave the Twingo. Clearly such a possibility hadn't crossed Monsieur Leclercq's mind. Thus spoke the man who had his own personal parking space at the office.

Driving round the perimeter of the Promenades Populle for a second time, Monsieur Pamplemousse was almost tempted to give it up as a bad job when he spotted a Renault Espace backing out from behind a building. Ignoring an arrow indicating exit only, he shot into the vacant space, just beating another driver who'd had his eyes on it too.

Four elderly ladies seated on a concrete bench broke off from their gossiping to watch. Clearly, had there been an argument they would have been only too pleased to join in.

Pommes Frites stirred in his sleep as the sound of the engine died away and he heard his master's door open and shut. Not having eaten since breakfast, he had a large hole in his stomach; a hole which had featured in a particularly good dream he'd been having; a dream in which bones played a major part; bones of all shapes, sizes and from a variety of sources. A dark patch on the rear seat bore mute testimony to their combined tastiness. (Fortunately it was covered in washable velour material since, although it was available in a wide range of colours, saliva grey was not among those listed.)

Torn between seeing what was going on outside the car and staying put for a little while longer, Pommes Frites chose the latter course and closed his eyes again.

His bliss was short-lived, for almost at once he

was brought to his feet by the peremptory voice barking out orders again. Not once, but several times in quick succession: 'STAND CLEAR. SYSTEM ARMED' followed by 'SYSTEM DISARMED', then 'SYSTEM ARMED'. It was all very confusing and for a few seconds he was up and down like the proverbial yo-yo.

During the course of one of his upward leaps, he happened to glance through the rear window and caught sight of his master. For some reason best known to himself Monsieur Pamplemousse was doing almost exactly the same thing; jumping up and down like a yo-yo. The only difference between the two of them was that he, Pommes Frites, was doing his best to obey orders, whereas his master appeared to be taking the opposite line. He was sucking his fingers and shouting *merde* at the top of his voice.

Not for the first time, Pommes Frites feared for his master's sanity. He was certainly very red in the face.

However, as is so often the case in life, the truth of the matter was much simpler. Monsieur Pamplemousse had discovered the hard way that the Twingo's exhaust pipe was smaller by at least one centimetre than the sum total of its keys plus the security triggering device. And since both were encumbered by a large rubber ball on the end of a chain, a ball which as far as he could see served no purpose whatsoever, what should have been a simple operation of pushing them up the exhaust pipe was rendered impossible.

And even if he had been able to carry out the task, the end of the pipe had a bend in it so that it faced downwards; something the Director, who wasn't noted for being mechanically minded, had clearly overlooked. (So unmechanically minded was Monsieur Leclercq, rumour had it that when his wife had asked him to check the oil in her Volkswagen, he'd telephoned the police to report the engine was missing. But since it was one of Glandier's stories and he had embroidered it still further by going on to say that luckily there had been a spare in the boot, the story had been taken with a large pinch of salt by the rest of the staff, although it went down well at the annual get-together.)

As Pommes Frites braced himself for his third journey into space, he felt a sudden jolt and the command 'STAND CLEAR' was repeated. It was followed by the high-pitched sound of a siren programmed to change its note every ten seconds or so.

Pommes Frites' literary bent didn't really extend much beyond recognising certain street signs like *CHIENS INTERDIT* (an example of which he was to come across all too soon, much to his master's dismay) and it certainly wasn't sufficiently advanced to allow him the luxury of following a series of illustrations. Had it been, a brief glance in the instruction manual would have made everything abundantly clear. Under a section headed 'Security' he would have come across the words: 'When a more serious aggressive impact occurs (and here the writer forebore to give as an example a well-directed kick making contact with a rear tyre) the voice message will be followed by a full circle of five distinctive and different siren tones – a powerful 120 decibels – to attract attention.'

It was certainly doing that. A fifth lady had already joined those on the bench, and a small crowd of passers-by had begun to collect on the pavement alongside the park. As with traffic entering the town, they seemed to be appearing as if from nowhere and more were emerging by the second from a café on the far side of the road.

An unmarked car drew up and two men in uniform climbed out. As they drew near, Monsieur Pamplemousse stopped massaging his big toe and tried to pull himself together.

'It is nothing,' he said, bending down to demonstrate his problem. 'I have burnt my fingers on the exhaust pipe, that is all.'

For the most part the crowd had been standing by in silence, awaiting developments, but then he heard some unmistakably English voices.

'Poor old thing . . . look at him.'

'Ought not to be allowed . . .'

'Bloody frogs!' The latter delivered in a tone of voice implying that at another time, in another place, a lynching party might be the order of the day.

Monsieur Pamplemousse glanced up in gratitude. How typical of the British! Defenders of the Faith. Champions of the underdog. Long may they live. What would the world do without them?

Meeting with a stony stare, he looked back over his shoulder and gave a start. His mind having been temporarily elsewhere, what he had taken to be the alarm system entering into a musical mode, rather more *agitato* than *andante con moto*, and far exceeding in decibels anything that had gone before was, in fact, the voice of woe *in extremis* and it was coming from inside the car.

'Well?' It was the red-faced individual again. 'Aren't you going to do something about him?'

Monsieur Pamplemousse glared back. He should have known. Perfidious Albions. Hypocrites all. Their professed love of animals often masked their real feelings; one of dislike for the French. No wonder they were responsible for mad cow disease and half the other ills in the world.

'*Monsieur* has travelled far?' the senior of the two officers broke into his reveries.

'From Paris.' Monsieur Pamplemousse prayed he wouldn't be asked to produce his licence. The fingers of his right hand felt as though they had been dipped in boiling oil.

'I simply wished to leave the keys inside the pipe for safe keeping,' he added briefly by way of explanation, as he went round the side of the car to open one of the doors; not a moment too soon in Pommes Frites' humble opinion.

'Lovely day for a long drive,' ventured the man's colleague, clearly playing the part of the nicer of the two.

'It's no wonder your exhaust is hot,' said the first. 'No doubt *Monsieur* made good time.'

Monsieur Pamplemousse glared at him. He wasn't falling for that old one, an approach much beloved of the traffic police.

'It is a new car,' he said stiffly. 'I drove slowly, for it needs to be treated with respect.'

The senior *gendarme* touched the brim of his hat. 'Have we met before, *Monsieur*?'

'I think not.'

Catching sight of Pommes Frites, recognition dawned in the officer's eyes. His face took on a look of respect as he automatically straightened his shoulders.

'If I can be of any assistance, Monsieur Pamplemousse.'

'*Non, merci.*' Monsieur Pamplemousse suppressed a sigh. He wished it hadn't happened, but it wasn't the first time. His picture had appeared in too many *journaux* over the years; whenever a particularly juicy case had hit the headlines, not to mention his own enforced early retirement following the scandal at the *Folies*. If the latter hadn't exactly stood him in good favour with those on high, at least it had made him a figure of renown in the lower ranks.

He glanced round at the crowd of onlookers. What was it the Director had said? '*Anonymat* at all times.' If he felt that way he might have chosen a car of a different colour. Anything less anonymous than a bright yellow Twingo, *jaune paille* as the makers chose to call it, would be hard to imagine. It stood out like a beacon in the car park. Sore thumb was not a comparison he wished to make at that moment.

Word would get around. Passers-by would be stopping to have a closer look for the rest of the day.

And if he did hang around in the hope that someone might turn up, who knew when that would be? It could be in half an hour. It could be late that evening. It might even be the following day.

Monsieur Pamplemousse changed his mind. 'I wish to make a telephone call,' he said. 'Meanwhile . . .' His brief, almost imperceptible nod towards the assembly was taken on board in a trice. It was part of the brotherhood, a kind of lesser Masonic lodge where a wink was as good as a secret handshake.

Reaching for his baton, the *gendarme* nodded in the direction of a group of three telephone boxes. 'Over there, *Monsieur*.'

'The ones in the front are the worst,' murmured Monsieur Pamplemousse as he signalled Pommes Frites to follow him. 'English animal rights protesters of the very worst kind.'

While he was feeding the machine he toyed with the idea of leaving a note up the exhaust pipe, saying where he could be found, but decided it might smoulder and catch fire, attracting even further attention.

Véronique answered his call straight away. It was as he feared. Monsieur Leclercq was not available.

'He is taking the chief of one of the press agencies out to lunch.'

He could guess which one *and* the subject under discussion.

'Can I help in any way?'

'Simply tell Monsieur LeClercq, "Mission Unaccomplished." He will understand.'

'*Oh là là!*' Véronique sounded alarmed. 'Are you all right, Monsieur Pamplemousse? Is there anything I can do to help?'

'Sadly, no,' said Monsieur Pamplemousse. 'I will try phoning him again when I reach Dulac.'

With a heavy heart Monsieur Pamplemousse returned to his car, closed the boot, signalled Pommes Frites to follow him and took his own place behind the steering wheel. Not wishing to miss any of the fun Pommes Frites clambered in beside him.

Settling himself down he wondered idly why they went out through the entry to the car park when other cars were queuing to get in. It didn't seem a very popular move.

One way and another his master seemed to be having one of 'those days'.

CHAPTER THREE

It was entirely his own fault. He shouldn't have stopped, but curiosity got the better of him; the same curiosity that had proverbially killed the cat, and in Monsieur Pamplemousse's case was to lead to the death of someone who happened to be in the wrong place at the wrong time.

It had started to snow soon after he left Roanne; at first only a few wispy flakes, then it grew heavier and more sustained. The sky looked full of it, and the few Charolais cattle that were still out and about were beginning to look grubby, as though they were all in need of a bath. Everything in life was relative, even different shades of white.

Passing through a small wood soon after beginning the long climb up to the Col de Buchet, he noticed someone had hacked out a patch of ground in a sheltered, south-facing clearing and planted cabbages. It was scratching a living with a vengeance, but hope springs eternal in the human breast.

He was still thinking about it when he entered a sharp right-hand bend and nearly collided with a small Citroën coming in the opposite direction. It was on the wrong side of the road and the grey-haired woman driver appeared affronted, as though he had no right to be there.

Taking a quick look in his rear-view mirror, he saw she had skidded to a stop and was reversing, rather as though she intended making a U-turn in order to come after him. Surely not, since she was so clearly in the wrong, cutting the corner in a manner typical of a local inhabitant claiming right of way. It could be that she wished to apologise for her error of judgement, but he rather doubted it.

Pulling in to the side of the road, he waited until the other car came alongside before opening his window.

'Monsieur Pamplemousse! I heard you were in the area. Then, when I saw the yellow Twingo . . .'

News had always travelled fast in the Auvergne, via the bush telegraph, grapevine, call it what you liked; in this day and age probably the Internet, it was all the same. You only had to breathe the magic words 'Don't tell anyone', and it spread like wildfire. Even so . . . this was ridiculous.

'You won't remember me. We were at school together.'

'Of course . . .' Monsieur Pamplemousse racked his brains, but he had totally no idea.

'Don't tell me you have forgotten the woodshed at the bottom of the playground. If you remember, I ran home and told Mama of your naughtiness and she wouldn't let me speak to you for the rest of that term.'

'Honoré!' Monsieur Pamplemousse stared at her as it all came back to him. The steel-rimmed glasses hadn't helped. She hadn't worn glasses of any kind in those far off days, although looking back he had always thought of her as being a bit short-sighted.

A finger wagged. 'You haven't changed. I read about that business at the *Folies*. Your reason for taking early retirement from the *Sûreté*.'

'You shouldn't believe everything you read in the *journaux*,' said Monsieur Pamplemousse gruffly. 'It was all a mistake. Someone was out to get me. Besides, they exaggerate. It wasn't the whole chorus line. Only a few.'

Realising he was wasting his breath, he tried changing the subject. 'What are you doing now?'

'I am the headmistress.'

Monsieur Pamplemousse gave a whistle. 'Little Honoré Pichot! Who would have believed it?' Well, he would have for a start. Even at the age of seven she had been a strict disciplinarian. Stealing a kiss had been something of a challenge at the time; a dare on the part of his classmates and one that had backfired as far as he was concerned, but they had all thought it a huge joke.

She was wearing thick driving gloves, but he would have bet anything they didn't conceal a ring.

'Madame Pichot . . .'

'*Mademoiselle*.' Her correction made it sound like a triumph of wisdom over the forces of evil. 'I cannot wait to tell the others you are here.'

'I would much rather you didn't,' said Monsieur Pamplemousse. Having stories about his early exploits bandied about, stories which doubtless had become heavily embroidered over the years, was the last thing he needed.

Mademoiselle Pichot didn't exactly say, 'What is it worth to keep quiet?' At least, not in so many words. The gleam in her eyes was enough.

Which was how he came to find himself being blackmailed – on reflection there was no other word for it – into agreeing to attend a prize-giving ceremony at his old school at eleven o'clock the following day.

'After all,' Mlle Pichot reverted to her role of headmistress, 'you *are* our most famous *vieux garçon*.'

At that moment a large *camion* laden with freshly

cut timber came up behind them and the driver gave a blast on his horn, impatient at having to stop. His action forced Monsieur Pamplemousse into making a snap decision before going on his way.

In the circumstances he could hardly have said 'no', but as he neared Pouligny he began to wish he'd at least made the attempt. So much for a quiet spell away from it all.

On entering the village his spirits sank still further. At first sight there was little left of the place as he remembered it. The fact that it now merited a bypass should have forewarned him. Everywhere there were signs of a new-found prosperity. The Twingo's tyres transmitted a warning rumble via the suspension as he passed a *Chaussée Cahoteuse* sign at speed and hit a series of humps in a road which had been relaid in red brick. Pommes Frites eyed him reproachfully in the rear-view mirror. Over the next hundred metres or so he encountered no less than three pedestrian crossings, all entirely devoid of human life, before a sign indicating a *Zone Scolaire* forced him to slow down still further. In his day going to school had been a case of waiting for the sound of approaching traffic, then making a dash for it; the first one across the road being labelled a sissy. They had never lost the last one to have a go.

Truly motorists were rapidly becoming an endangered species. Pariahs of the very worst kind, sent packing the long way round whenever possible.

Entering what had once been the market square he saw the statue to Louis XIV had been moved to one side, its place taken by a *rond-point* of all things. The old horse trough where on fête days the wandering minstrel had set up his ten-stringed hurdy-gurdy was nowhere to be seen. Probably in some antique store where it would end its days as a garden ornament.

The opposite side of the square had been laid out as a parking area, empty now apart from a van and a scooter, both covered in a layer of snow. It was curiosity again that caused Monsieur Pamplemousse to park the Twingo alongside them and climb out in order to take stock of his surroundings. And once again, when he had time to view everything in retrospect, he had cause to wonder what would have happened had he bypassed the village altogether. It was one of those moments which confirmed his belief that some things in life felt as though they were preordained, with everything fitting into place like a jigsaw puzzle.

The old round-domed Romanesque church just off the square was still in place, exactly as he remembered it, and indeed exactly as it had been since the establishment of the Capetian kingdom in the eleventh century.

In direct contrast, posters outside a *tabac* invited

him to dance the *Chaud Chaud* in *Le Club*. As an added attraction between numbers, for one week only, a hypnotist was appearing.

The Café du Commerce was still there, much as he remembered it, except for a large espresso coffee machine dominating the zinc bar. A group of old men stared out at him as he walked past. He wondered if he had known some of them as a small boy. More to the point, had any of them known him, and would they recognise him?

The answer came almost immediately as they all waved in unison.

When he was safely free of their gaze he paused to look at his own reflection in a shop window. Surely he didn't look quite as old as they did? At least he wasn't waiting the end of his life away in a café bar. Thank goodness he had left when he did.

The *bricolage* was still there; old Pascal the owner – if he was still alive he must be at least ninety by now – must have dug his heels in. Entering it had always been a treat. He wondered if it still smelt of old leather hunting jackets and tarred rope: it had been a treasure house of dog chains, screws, nails, nuts and bolts, fencing; anything and everything to do with the countryside. And if it wasn't in stock it would arrive the next day by the ancient delivery van that plied between the village and Roanne until the war eventually put a stop to it.

Those few things aside, the village of Pouligny might well have been renamed Dulacsville. Most three Stock Pot establishments had irons in other fires these days – the state of the economy dictated it – but Dulac had really pulled out all the stops.

Sandwiched between the old *Crédit Mutuel*, now sporting a gleaming new façade, and a kitchen shop with cookery books elegantly displayed alongside gleaming pots and pans and other culinary equipment, there was a boutique displaying what he assumed were the latest fashions. It was a far cry from old Madame Armoury (Late of Paris and Rome); rumour always had it that she had only been to those two places while on holiday.

Without moving another step he could see a smart winery, a *pâtisserie*, its windows full of pastries and jars of *confiture*, a delicatessen, the carefully restored remains of the original hotel, now turned into a museum and a hair-dressing salon.

Trade was not brisk in any of the shops; a sprinkling of Japanese and some Germans in the boutique – the former probably on the lookout for Hermès scarves and ties; some Americans were browsing in the kitchen shop; an English couple were gazing in awe at the window of the *pâtisserie*. It wasn't hard to identify the different nationalities.

He wondered what the local inhabitants thought of it all. Doubtless it had been part of the deal that in return for Dulac getting planning permission, all the roads and pavements had been relaid at his expense. The old guard would be up in arms, the younger generation probably embraced the arrival of a hairdressing salon and a hi-fi shop, for unlike many such places in the Auvergne, which over the years had seen the population dwindle, that of Pouligny must have increased threefold.

And then, a short way along the street leading out of the square, on the other side of a tiny stream that ran through the village, a tributary of the Loire – when he was small he'd thought it was the Loire itself – he came across another anachronism: slap, bang, where it had always been and badly in need of a coat of paint, looking for all the world like an abandoned film set, stood the Hôtel du Commerce. He remembered it well. In its day it had been a rival to the Hôtel Moderne, the forerunner of Dulac.

Monsieur Pamplemousse supposed people must stay there still, perhaps the odd commercial traveller trying to save on his expenses. Welcome wasn't exactly written in large letters on the mat, but then it never had been.

As he drew near he glanced at a menu held inside in a glass-covered board by the entrance. Undated, it had an air of permanency about it. What must once have been written in dark blue was now purple with age. It was also very predictably a menu of the region, founded on ham, eggs and cheese. A choice between roast pork with chestnuts *à la clermontois*, pig's trotters with lentils and Cantal cheese, or *Truffade auvergnate* – cheese, bacon and potato pancakes, followed by the ubiquitous *clafoutis* – tiny black cherries cooked in batter. Wine included – thirty francs. To anyone as hungry as he was beginning to feel, it made tempting reading (and on the face of it, not bad value), but he wondered.

The hotel had never made *Le Guide*, or any other gastronomic publication as far as he knew. It had been owned by another branch of the Dulac family; someone who called himself Claude Le Auvergnat, and in truth Claude had never been rated very highly as a chef. Authentic recipes they may have been, but they lacked the one essential ingredient, love. The local name for indigestion had been 'an attack of the Claudes'. Even in his own day, when Claude's father had been in charge, it had always been a case of take it or leave it.

It was the other side of the Dulac family who had all the talent; the talent and the ambition to go with it. All around him stood living proof of that.

Monsieur Pamplemousse reached for the notebook he kept concealed in a pocket of his right trouser leg. There was no harm in adding to his store of knowledge. As he removed his Cross pen from an inner pocket and stood poised to write, a sixth sense made him aware that someone was watching him through a gap in the net curtains. He stood for a moment, pretending to be lost in thought, then suddenly looked round, but whoever it was must have read his thoughts and anticipated accordingly. The curtains fell back into place before he had a chance to catch sight of who was behind them.

It was probably only his imagination, but as he made his way back down the street to where he had left the Twingo, Monsieur Pamplemousse felt a prickling sensation down the back of his spine. He was determined not to give way to it and look back. Ever sensitive to his master's moods, Pommes Frites suffered no such inhibitions. He hung around the hotel entrance for a while as though expecting something to happen and when it didn't he left his mark before he went on his way wearing one of his enigmatic expressions. A keen observer might have noted that he didn't bother leaving any further marks *en route* as was his usual wont, although given the fact that nothing had passed his lips since early morning that wasn't so surprising.

Each lost in their own thoughts, they stayed that way as Monsieur Pamplemousse doubled back on himself and after a brief excursion round the rest of the village, drove out of Pouligny following the signs to Dulac. He passed a small working quarry, rounded a bend in the road and there it was spread out before him.

In strictly family terms, the contrast between the old guard and the new could scarcely have been greater: the one seedy and down at heel; the other, perched on the side of a hill a kilometre or so outside the village at the end of a narrow, purpose-built tarmac road; chic, modern, forward-looking.

Viewed from a distance it looked more like a fictional space laboratory than a hotel; mostly single-storied, but with a large domed main building in the middle, rather as though it had been conceived by an architect from a catalogue of parts, instead of starting from scratch on a drawing board. Perhaps it had been, but Monsieur Pamplemousse couldn't help wondering what its shelf life would be. The call nowadays was for something new, and built-in obsolescence wasn't the sole prerogative of the automobile industry, but it was no wonder the local authorities had screwed Dulac into the ground before granting planning permission.

The only sign of life came from a flock of birds suddenly rising into the air as a man emerged from an area of beech trees to his left. Weaving an unsteady path, he picked his way across a small stream cascading down the hill; a tributary of the tributary that flowed through the village, one of the many thousands that eventually ended up as the mighty Loire when it reached the sea in Brittany.

Whether it was the snow or he had been drinking was impossible to say; perhaps a bit of each, for he was making slow progress. He had a canvas bag over one shoulder, and Pommes Frites pricked up his ears at the sight of a large black dog ambling along behind, making the most of the snow. They must have been together, yet they looked strangely apart. The whole thing, the presence of water and cover, two basic necessities for the survival of wildlife, the behaviour of the man and his dog, made Monsieur Pamplemousse suspect a poacher at work, although the man didn't seem to be making any bones about it. He might have owned the place.

Further up the hill a pair of imposing wrought-iron gates set beneath a stone archway bore the single word DULAC in gold lettering, marking the entrance to the grounds. As they drew near he heard a warning blast of a siren, and braking sharply, drew into the side of the road. Seconds later an ambulance poked its nose through the opening, gave another wail, then swept past them, heading back down the hill towards the village.

It was once again partly a case of cause and effect, but the brief encounter was sufficient to allow them time to see a sign which they might

77

otherwise have missed. Poking up out of the snow just inside the gates was a small board bearing a picture of a dog. Pommes Frites eyed it gloomily, not so much because it was an artist's impression, and in his opinion a very poor one at that – some kind of terrier by the look of it – but because the features were partly obliterated by a large red line.

Monsieur Pamplemousse's reaction was more of a double take. He could hardly believe his eyes. It was something else Monsieur Leclercq hadn't taken into account; segregation of the very worst kind, the canine equivalent of apartheid. Worse still, it was probably done as a sop to foreign tourists who objected to seeing animals in the dining room. *CHIENS INTERDIT* indeed! Where else did they expect them to eat? What was the world coming to?

Well, it certainly wasn't going to stop him staying there. Pommes Frites would have to remain in the car for the time being and be smuggled in through a back door. If there was such a thing as a back door at Dulac.

They drove in silence past a helicopter landing pad, then a sign pointing the way toward a nine-hole golf course. Despite the snow, a small group of hardy Japanese in red Wellington boots were at the first tee practising their putting with a black ball. Monsieur Pamplemousse shivered. It reminded him of Boulogne. From a distance their matching red umbrellas with the single letter 'D' in blue added a colourful touch to the scene and he was almost tempted to stop and take a photograph. Cartier-Bresson would have clicked his shutter long ago and forgotten all about it, except of course his were always in black and white. Had he ever used colour? He couldn't recall seeing any.

Otherwise there didn't appear to be anyone around. Apart from playing golf in the snow, he wondered what people did all day.

Now that he was near enough to take a closer look, he saw that the layout of the hotel was not dissimilar to that of an airport, with corridors radiating out from the central area like the spokes of a cartwheel. Every spoke had attached to it a series of satellite rooms, each with its own patio arranged in such a way that it wasn't overlooked by its immediate neighbour. In summer the views must be magnificent.

Some of the rooms had a car parked outside, and in addition to the internal corridor all were reached by a small ring road which clearly had the benefit of underground heating, for it was devoid of snow. Perhaps he had misjudged the architect after all, for he seemed to have thought of everything.

Another sign pointed to an underground car park. Across the entrance there was a police car, its doors still open as though the occupants had arrived in a hurry. Monsieur Pamplemousse parked alongside it, so that he was shielded from the main entrance to the hotel. He didn't want some young commis waiter on baggage duty to discover Pommes Frites before he'd had time to check out the lie of the land. Valet parking could be another hazard.

He needn't have worried. Luck was with him. As he entered the reception area he found all eyes were on the departure desk where a major row was in progress. Snatches of it reached his ears: more monologue than dialogue since it seemed to be entirely one-sided; a no holds barred assault on the part of a woman of uncertain age and a small group behind the counter. It wasn't hard to tell who was winning. Short, fat, her immaculately coiffeured head barely reached above the counter, but what she lacked in height she made up for in volume.

'Doesn't anyone here speak plain English?' she demanded. 'I want you to know I'm having it removed. You know why? It's going to be exhibit 'A' in the lawsuit I'm bringing just as soon as Melvin and I get back home.'

The thought of having whatever it was removed brought a fresh murmur of protest.

'Forget it. I got pictures. Just you wait until you get the bill from Melv's orthodontist! *And* I'm taking you to the cleaners for stress, loss of dignity, loss of amenities through having to cut short our holiday . . . you name it. And that's without the phone bill. You won't know what hit you . . .' A peremptory call for the bell captain brought the diatribe to an end as she ran out of fingers.

An almost audible sigh of relief went up round the room. Two anonymous men in dark overcoats – local bankers or businessmen by the look of them; they might even have been tax collectors – rose to their feet and eyed Monsieur Pamplemousse as he went past, hastily circumnavigated a trolley piled high with Louis Vuitton luggage, then wormed his way between three police officers, two in uniform, one in plain clothes, who had been standing well clear of the argument.

Their leader, short, stocky, greying hair cut short in military fashion, was a typical detective of the old school. He looked as though he might have been about to say something, but then thought better of it when he heard Monsieur Pamplemousse checking in under the name of Blanc.

Monsieur Pamplemousse held his breath while the receptionist made an impression of his CIC credit card. It wouldn't be an ideal moment to have her spot his deliberate mistake, but he needn't have worried. She clearly couldn't wait to talk to her colleagues on the other desk.

'*Pardon, Monsieur.*' Pressing a button to summon help, she handed back his card. 'I will have Shinko direct you to your room. I hope you enjoy your stay with us.'

Expecting someone of Asian extraction, a Japanese girl perhaps, since Dulac had not long ago returned from one of his Far Eastern excursions bearing a blushing bride, Monsieur Pamplemousse was taken by surprise when a tall, dark-haired girl, elegantly dressed in a black trouser-suit and bow tie, materialised by his side. She took a key from her colleague and looked at him enquiringly.

'My valise is still in the car,' said Monsieur Pamplemousse by way of explanation, as he led the way outside. 'Shinko? You are from Japan?'

'No,' said the girl. 'Knightsbridge, actually.'

'Ah, so you are English.'

The girl nodded as she climbed in to the passenger seat. 'It was Mummy's idea.'

'Mama's have such ideas the world over.' Monsieur Pamplemousse started the engine and followed her directions along the ring road.

'Shinko means "a growing girl". It was in memory of Daddy. He fell in the Yangste soon after I was born and he was never seen again. They say he trod on a crocodile.'

Monsieur Pamplemousse gave the girl a sideways glance. It was hard to tell if she was being serious or not. That was the trouble with the English. They treated everything as though it were some kind of joke. Did they have crocodiles in the Yangste? He decided to drop the subject.

'So what was all the trouble about? And what is being removed as exhibit "A"?'

'There's been a nasty ax in the gym.'

'An ax in the gym. *Qu'est-ce que c'est?*'

'Sorry. An accident in the Physical Tuning Centre. There was a spot of bother with one of the velos – the cycling machines. She'll have a job taking it away. It's bolted to the concrete.'

'And that brought the police in?'

'It isn't the first time the jinx has struck. Except it isn't a jinx. Jinxes don't saw through . . .' She seemed only too eager to discuss the matter. 'I'm sorry, I don't know the French for those things that hold the bits the pedals are attached to . . . the crank . . . to the gear wheel that drives the chain.' She broke off and gave a laugh. 'It sounds like a song . . .'

'I think you mean the *clavettes*,' ventured Monsieur Pamplemousse.

'Brilliant.'

'A good many Frenchmen wouldn't know that either. So what happened?'

'Suite 22 was having a last go before checking out. It's on video. All the machines have separate cameras so that the results can be recorded and afterwards you get given a printout. Apparently he was pedalling away like mad. He'd got up to nearly forty kilometres an hour when both whatever it was you called them snapped at the same time. Wham! Half his teeth are on the floor, the rest are still stuck to the handlebars. They say there's even one embedded in the camera lens. Talk about Doomsville!'

'*Sacrebleu!*'

'The French have a word for it,' began the girl, then nearly jumped out of her skin as Pommes Frites stirred in the back seat at the sound of his master's voice.

'Forgive me,' said Monsieur Pamplemousse. 'I should have warned you.' He reached inside his jacket. 'Are you good at keeping secrets? Between ourselves, I have a small problem. His name is Pommes Frites.'

'A large one if you ask me.' Shinko eyed Pommes Frites nervously as he stood up and peered over her shoulder.

'Take this . . .'

She held up a hand. 'It's very kind of you, but it isn't necessary. Save it for the room maid. You may need it. Word gets around.'

'Please,' insisted Monsieur Pamplemousse. 'I would be grateful for your help and it will make me much happier.'

With a becoming blush the girl folded the note

and slipped it into a top pocket of her jacket. At the same time she directed him into a parking bay outside one of the apartments.

Leading the way across the patio she opened a sliding glass door, then stood back to allow the others entry. Leaving Pommes Frites to carry out an inspection of his new surroundings while the girl got his luggage from the boot, Monsieur Pamplemousse squeezed past a white table and matching chairs. One thing was certain. He wouldn't be having *petit déjeuner* outside next morning.

Entering the lounge area of the suite he found himself surrounded on all sides by understated elegance. In front of a long grey leather sofa there was a low table on top of which, alongside a telephone, reposed a bowl of fresh fruit and beside that another, smaller bowl containing chocolates from Bernachon in Lyon. At the other end there was an arrangement of flowers in Japanese minimalist fashion; three out-of-season tulips standing to attention in a thin glass vase.

Opening the door to a cupboard opposite the sofa he found a large television receiver with a separate video recorder, a fax machine with instructions for personalising the dial-in number, and let into the wall, a small safe, again with personal coding facilities.

While he was waiting for Shinko to return with

his baggage he carried out a quick inspection of the rest of the apartment.

The bathroom, situated between the lounge and the bedroom, was an architect's dream of stainless steel, marble and smoked glass. There were mirrors everywhere, presumably to make you feel good or bad depending on how the fancy took you. Everything had been thought of: hairdryer; supply of tissues; two dressing gowns in his and her sizes; a plentiful supply of oils and soaps by Nina Ricci. Face cloths; a profusion of towels in various sizes, all monogrammed with a large letter D.

And why not? André Dulac had every reason to be proud of his achievement. To have created such an oasis in a normally remote part of France so that people from the world over flocked there all the year round was no mean feat.

He wondered what Doucette would have thought of the glass doors to each of the separate cubicles containing the bidet and the shower. There would be an *'Oh là là!'* or two.

The sunken bath was approached via three marble steps, and behind a glass-panelled wall at its foot he could see a second television receiver in the bedroom, this time on a swivel base so that it could be turned to face whoever was in the bath.

Entering the next room, Monsieur Pamplemousse

tested the springiness of the vast double bed with his hand, then lay back for a moment taking stock of his surroundings. He could get used to this and no mistake. Pommes Frites would be in his element when he saw it.

On either side of him there were stainless steel panels let into the wall. Closer inspection revealed several rows of buttons controlling the roller blinds, not only in the bedroom itself, but in the other rooms as well. Other buttons operated the lighting system in seemingly endless variations and combinations, as well as the television with its combined video player. Separate knobs controlled temperature and humidity, and as far as he could tell the air conditioning was mercifully silent. On a bad day you need never get up.

It was a wonder they didn't make sure you had a degree in electronics before they allowed you in.

Hearing noises coming from the other room he retraced his steps to the sitting room.

'I'm sorry we've been such a long time,' said Shinko. 'For some reason best known to himself, Pommes Frites fancied a walk in the snow. He seemed to have a lot of investigating to do.'

'Sometimes,' said Monsieur Pamplemousse, 'he plays his cards close to his chest. He didn't spend several years in the Paris *Sûreté for* nothing.'

'Pommes Frites was in the Paris *Sûreté?*'

'We both were,' said Monsieur Pamplemousse proudly. 'He only left because he was made redundant following a cutback. It was my good fortune that it happened at the same time as I took early retirement and they gave him to me as a leaving present. In his time he was sniffer dog of the year. He won the Pierre Armand Golden Bone trophy.'

'Brilliant!' The girl gazed at them both with new respect. 'I tell you something, though. He'll have to do something about wiping his paws when he comes in. Just look at the trails he's left.'

'He is tired,' said Monsieur Pamplemousse. 'We both are. We have had a long journey. I wonder . . . would it be possible to order something? A steak for Pommes Frites and a sandwich or two.'

'Of course. All things are possible.' She glanced down at Pommes Frites.

'*À point?*'

Monsieur Pamplemousse shook his head and reached for his wallet again. 'Given the choice, he prefers it *saignant.*'

Shinko gave a sudden frown – almost like a nervous tic. 'This time it really isn't necessary.' She was gone before he had time to argue.

Left to his own devices Monsieur Pamplemousse picked up the nearest telephone, dialled 9 for an outside line, and tried calling Doucette. There was no answer. Either she was out shopping or she had gone to see her sister in Melun.

He had no better luck with the Director.

Véronique was *désolée*. 'He left early. He's been like a cat on hot bricks all day. You could try reaching him on his mobile. He was asking earlier if you had rung in yet.'

Monsieur Pamplemousse glanced at his watch. It was approaching the hour of *affluence* and he had no wish to embark on long explanations if Monsieur Leclercq was battling with the rush hour traffic. He had a habit of disappearing into tunnels just at the crucial moment and then being tetchy when he came out the other end having missed half the conversation.

'If he asks again, tell him I'm at the hotel and I'll try later.'

Feeling strangely deflated, Monsieur Pamplemousse switched on the television and set about doing his unpacking.

Picking up the remote control, he flipped through the channels as he came and went. There was nothing he wanted to see. The Sports Channel was showing tennis from goodness knew where. Not only was the world shrinking at an alarming rate, seasonal joys were fast becoming a thing of the past.

The Movie Channel was showing a film he had seen with Doucette at least ten years ago. A magazine programme was full of people airing their views about nothing of any great importance; more for their own enjoyment than anyone else's. It was no wonder the Americans, always good for the apt phrase, called it surfing. Skimming the surface in the hope of finding something worthwhile in the murky waters. It was one area where more definitely wasn't better.

He had more luck with the refrigerator. Champagne bearing the name Dulac, a plain and a rosé; red and white wine in quarter litre bottles. All the usual miniatures of spirits. Several cans of Heineken and Carlsberg beer. Three varieties of water including one from the Monts des Vosges; Wattwiller. *Rare et Bienfaisante.* He jotted down the name. It was a useful way of gaining the ascendancy if you encountered a wine waiter who needed taking down a cru or two. An assortment of nuts and other comestibles.

He was about to pour himself a beer when there was a knock on the outer door leading to the corridor. He opened it and Shinko entered pushing a serving trolley.

'Sorry I've been so long. The kitchen's busy what with everyone being inside because of the snow. I had to organise it myself.' She lifted a silver dome '. . . One large *entrecôte* steak, *saignant*, for Pommes Frites . . .' then pointed to another plate bearing an oblong loaf of brown bread standing on end. It was of the style sold by the English firm Marks & Spencer in their Paris establishment and currently much in favour. What they called a 'tin' loaf in the quaint way the English had of describing things.

'Hey presto!' Removing the top crust she revealed that the inside had been removed so that it formed a hollow shell in which to contain the crustless sandwiches. 'Brilliant! I asked for an assortment.'

It was the kind of touch that separated the men from the boys; the three Stock Pot establishments from the mere two. Even when the pressures were on nothing was too much trouble.

'*And . . .*' Having spread a white napkin on the floor, Shinko returned to the trolley, opened a cupboard door in the base and took out two pairs of tiny Wellington boots. 'I've brought these for "a certain person". I dare say he'll want to go out after he's finished his snack.'

Clearly Pommes Frites had lost no time establishing a bond. Who was it said the English weren't a nation of pet lovers? All the same, Monsieur Pamplemousse eyed them dubiously. He strongly suspected the so-called 'certain person' might have his own views on the matter, but as if to give lie to the thought, while the girl was quickly and expertly cutting his steak into bite-size pieces, Pommes Frites gave the boots an approving sniff.

'Better safe than sorry,' said Shinko, transferring the plate to the napkin. 'Anyway, there are no children staying here at the moment so "Cloaks" won't miss them. *Bonne chance.*'

Once again she gave a nervous giggle and disappeared before Monsieur Pamplemousse had a chance to thank her, by which time Pommes Frites was already deeply into his steak.

Monsieur Pamplemousse didn't even bother trying to compete. Instead, he began working his way slowly through the sandwiches. He counted seven layers in all; neatly cut into quarter segments and containing in turn, *pâté*, smoked salmon, cream cheese with thinly sliced pickled gherkin, *écrevisse* lettuce and mayonnaise, ham, scrambled egg with tiny slivers of truffle . . .

Entering the list into his notebook reminded him in no uncertain terms once again of the burns on his fingertips. Holding the ice-cold cans of Carlsberg helped, but it would be a day or two before they returned to normal.

Ringing through to reception he left a message telling them he didn't want to be disturbed until further notice. To make doubly certain he hung the room card outside the door. It said PLEASE DO NOT DISTURB in no less than twenty-four different languages, some of which he could only hazard a wild guess at.

Operating the roller blinds in the bedroom he sat on the bed for a moment or two contemplating what he might have for his evening meal. To begin with, truffles would definitely be top of the list. It was nearing the end of the season and he might as well make the most of things. A simple omelette to begin with? Or perhaps as a *Julienne* mixed in with the beaten egg, returned to the shell and baked? On the other hand, and to his way of thinking it was still the best method of all, sliced and served on top of coarsely mashed potato coated with olive oil.

And to follow . . . he lay back and closed his eyes while he considered the matter. To follow . . .

When Monsieur Pamplemousse woke it was to the sound of Pommes Frites making one of his snuffling noises. It was the kind he held in reserve for times of emergency and it was coming from the other room. Guided by a flashing red light on the bedside telephone, he felt for the nearest bank of buttons. Having eventually located one for the room light, he operated the shutter. Raising it a little, he saw it was already dark outside. Dark and snowing hard. His heart sank when he looked at his watch. It was long past dinner time. He'd slept for well over six hours. It was no wonder Pommes Frites sounded restive.

Making his way into the other room, he was met by a pair of reproachful eyes. He set to work quickly. The boots slipped on easily enough and actually stayed in place, almost as though they had been made to measure.

It wasn't until he closed the French windows and Pommes Frites had hurried off into the night in search of the nearest tree that Monsieur Pamplemousse noticed an envelope had been slipped under the main door while he'd been asleep; several envelopes, in fact. The slips inside all said the same thing and they were timed at hourly intervals. The first at 18.30, the last 21.30. There was a message for him on the voicemail.

'Pamplemousse . . .' Once again the voice was slightly muffled, as though the Director didn't wish to be overheard. 'Pamplemousse, I fear the worst. What *is* going on?' He could have asked the same question. 'I know you are there. I have checked with reception. Please get in touch as soon as possible, but not, repeat *not* under any circumstances after 22.30. I promised Chantal an early night.'

Monsieur Pamplemousse checked his watch again and hesitated. Should he or should he not? It was already 22.40. Monsieur Leclercq was a stickler for accuracy. If he said not after 22.30 – he meant not after 22.30. But . . . other matters began to exercise his mind. Fancy missing his dinner on the very first night! He eyed the remains of the loaf of bread. At least he wouldn't starve. There was still the bowl of fruit to fall back on, not to mention the chocolate . . . On the other hand there were two mouths to feed. It would be a case of calling on room service again and without knowing how to get in contact with the girl he would have to wait until Pommes Frites returned so that he could hide him somewhere, although with so much in the way of glass partitioning it was hard to know exactly where. The need to hide a large bloodhound was something the architect hadn't thought of. Open planning was all very well in its place, but it did have its disadvantages.

Crossing to the window he looked out. It was black as pitch outside. Not a star to be seen. There was no sign of Pommes Frites either; only two sets of tiny footprints heading out into the night. The snow had eased off a little, and no doubt he would turn up when it suited him. In Paris he often went out for long periods at a time, and having been cooped up all day he was probably taking full advantage of being let out. In the meantime . . .

Monsieur Pamplemousse turned on the television again, but he wasn't in the mood. He felt restless. Having come away in a hurry he'd brought nothing with him to read and the hotel brochure only told him things he had already mostly discovered for himself.

He felt almost tempted to go for a walk. If the hotel kept Wellington boots for children they must surely have an ample supply for adults. On the other hand . . . he looked out of the window and decided against it.

A foray in the refrigerator yielded a packet of mixed nuts and a choice between champagne and a Heineken. Choosing a Heineken, he was about to flip the metal opener when the feeling came over him that he was being watched and looking up he saw a face pressed against the French windows.

Monsieur Pamplemousse's pleasure at seeing his friend and mentor return to the fold lasted all of five seconds. As Pommes Frites removed his nose from the glass and stood back wagging his tail in anticipation of the door being opened, he left behind an ominous dark stain. A stain which, to the trained eye, was immediately recognisable.

Blood was blood, no matter which way you looked at it.

CHAPTER FOUR

In the beginning it had been kisses all the way. Kisses to welcome him on his arrival. Kisses both before and after a Suze; rather more after it than before, and tasting strongly of gentian. Then kisses, brief but noticeably more lingering as they took a shortcut through the shrubbery on their way from the offices to the new school building.

And that had just been Mlle Pichot!

Honoré Pichot was certainly making up for her lost moments in the woodshed. Perhaps it was the after-effects of a long, hard winter with only the television for company; a combination calculated to underline the passage of time and engender restlessness in the most sanguine of souls. Whatever the cause, formality had been cast to one side. He was no longer Monsieur Pamplemousse, but Aristide. Soon it would be *tu* rather than *vous*, although not if he had any say in the matter. He couldn't help but notice a strong smell of perfume and her *décolleté* left little to the imagination. And was it imagination that caused him to suspect her glasses were a little steamed up? If so, it wasn't the only thing.

Fortunately the woodshed was no longer there. The spot where it had been was now given over to a large car park, otherwise there was no knowing what might have happened.

They walked in silence for a while, each busy with their own thoughts.

The new school was nothing like the one Monsieur Pamplemousse remembered of old. Built in 1885 on Republican ideals, the old one had originally been part of the *Mairie*, as was common practice in those days. The new building, brash and modern, occupied what had once been an area of wasteland behind it.

And that was another thing. Times change, but the parking area was packed with vehicles: cars, mopeds and various other forms of transport, including an invalid carriage.

'Not,' Honoré hastened to inform him, 'that they *all* belong to the pupils.' Some were owned by members of staff, parents and other interested parties who had come to meet him.

The car park had been given to the school by

Monsieur Dulac himself. 'Such a kind and generous person. Many of our ex-pupils have gone on to work for him.'

'I bet they have,' thought Monsieur Pamplemousse. 'It must have been a very good investment.'

His heart sank as he glanced through the windows of the new building and caught sight of a crowded hall. Heads were turned expectantly in his direction. More than ever he wished he hadn't agreed to the whole thing. The Director would not be pleased, it was a mercy he wasn't there to see him; all his worst fears would have been realised.

As it was, conversation that morning hadn't been easy. One-sided would have summed it up. Clearly, for reasons he wasn't prepared to reveal, Monsieur Leclercq had spent a sleepless night.

'Profiles, Pamplemousse, must be kept low,' had been his final enjoinder. 'Stay exactly where you are. Don't move. I will put "Plan B" into action from this end.'

Since Monsieur Pamplemousse had been taking a bath at the time, he'd felt justified in stretching matters a bit. If the Director didn't want him to meet the recipient of the car, then so be it. It was no skin off his nose. He saw no point in making a great production number out of it.

All the same, one way and another he was glad he had fortified himself afterwards over a good breakfast, otherwise the whole situation would have been hard to cope with. Glandier had spoken nothing less then the truth when he pronounced breakfast at Dulac as one of the best he had ever eaten; worthy of three Stock Pots in its own right. It was no mere trayload of *petit déjeuner* that had been delivered to his room that morning. It arrived on a *chariot* and more than made up for the previous evening's *débâcle*.

On the bottom level of the trolley there had been a selection of the day's *journaux*. Much to his relief a quick flip through them revealed no follow-up of his escapade in Boulogne. The Director must have done his stuff. Anyway, by now it would be yesterday's news. Perhaps even more importantly, there had been no mention in the local *journal* of any untoward happenings during the night at Dulac, although at one stage he'd heard plenty of comings and goings, and the sound of slamming car doors. Raising the shutters slightly he'd seen several flashing blue lights and he wondered whether there had been another mishap in the gym. Later, there had been the sound of a helicopter landing and taking off again.

Then had come the equivalent of a bucket of cold water; the ice-cold *douche*. Tucked inside a separate wallet he found an envelope addressed to Monsieur Blanc. Inside it there had been a slightly worrying note from Shinko. Written in a schoolgirl hand, it said: 'Watch out! Inspector Lafarge has spotted your guilty secret. Dreadful news about "You know who". Take care! Love to P.F. See you . . .'

Cryptic was hardly the word for it. What guilty secret? Or, perhaps, to be more precise, which guilty secret? And he had totally no idea of 'who' the girl was referring to or what the dreadful news could be.

He had looked for her in reception after breakfast, but a party of half a dozen or so Americans had just arrived in a people carrier and all she had managed was a passing wave, so he was still none the wiser.

He followed Mlle Pichot up a short flight of steps and into the entrance hall of the new building. It was a shock as he entered it to find his photograph everywhere.

'I did warn you,' she said roguishly. 'You *are* our most famous ex-pupil.' At least she didn't use the term 'old'. 'Such a pity you had to retire early; just when you were at your peak. We used to keep scrapbooks of all your activities.'

Excusing herself for a moment, Mlle Pichot disappeared into a nearby office leaving him to dwell on his visage in its many forms over the years. She hadn't been joking. He could hardly believe his eyes. To all intents and purposes he was standing in a hall of fame; his own fame, or ill-fame, since there was even a picture taken shortly after his unhappy affair at the *Folies*; the one that in the end led to his early retirement.

He wondered if it was a permanent display, or whether it had been hastily put together for his benefit. Moving a picture frame to one side revealed an area of lighter cream paint, which answered the question. Wonders would never cease.

'*Alors*,' Honoré returned carrying a large silver cup, 'I have a little favour to ask of you, Aristide. This is for you to present to another ex-pupil. A little younger than yourself, but one of our rising young stars. A real all-rounder and a credit to us all. She has come back today especially to receive it. With your permission we plan to call it the "Aristide Pamplemousse Award" and make it an annual event.'

'It will be a pleasure,' said Monsieur Pamplemousse, with a graciousness he was far from feeling.

Following Honoré Pichot down a corridor he snatched a quick glance at his reflection in a mirror. There were no telltale traces of lipstick on his collar; a minor miracle considering all he had been through. Apart from a slightly drawn appearance there was little outward sign of the turmoil he felt within.

'*Bonne chance*, Aristide. Everyone is so looking forward to your speech.' Monsieur Pamplemousse came down to earth with a bump. He had been so taken up with his thoughts he'd become quite oblivious to what was going on around him.

Honoré Pichot fluttered her eyelashes as best she could. Like her smile, they were much as he remembered them, small and thin. 'I do so admire you men of the world who can address the multitude without so much as a single note.'

Monsieur Pamplemousse stared at her. '*Mais* . . .' he began. But he might just as well have saved his breath. A curtain was drawn to one side, and he found himself gently but firmly being ushered forward.

Following on behind, and reverting to her role of headmistress, Mlle Pichot held up her hand to quell the applause, tapped a microphone in the centre of the stage, then beckoned to someone in the front row.

'Claude, *s'il vous plaît.*'

There was another round of applause, this time rather more muted.

Monsieur Pamplemousse blinked in the spotlight. Not for the first time, he felt a touch of envy for Pommes Frites. Pommes Frites had things all worked out. There he was, blissfully sleeping off his breakfast in the back seat of the Twingo parked in the main square, totally oblivious to the problems of this world. Not that he wouldn't have taken the whole thing in his stride had he been there. Doubtless everyone would have wanted to stroke him for a start, which would have provided a welcome diversion. As it was . . .

As it was, having expected to see a small boy – probably the one with rimless glasses and a knowing air who had been staring at him without blinking ever since he'd arrived on stage – Monsieur Pamplemousse was taken aback to see a girl instead. And not just any old girl, but one that Glandier, an acknowledged expert in these matters, would have rated as being small, but perfectly formed.

She was wearing a tight miniskirt, an even tighter sweater and large black boots of a style he remembered his father wearing. As she drew near he became aware of the smell of jasmine. Close to, it was even more potent than Mlle Pichot's; tantalisingly so. A heady, sensual sensation. What was the figure he'd once had quoted at him when he'd been working a case involving passing off? One metric ton of flower petals, or eight million flowers, were needed for every two pounds of the perfume. He was certainly getting value for money.

Exactly why the girl was getting an award, and for what, Monsieur Pamplemousse had no idea, so he essayed a wild guess. 'For your outstanding work in many fields,' he began.

The titter which went round the first few rows of the audience was instantly quelled by Mlle Pichot.

As he shook the recipient's hand Monsieur

Pamplemousse gave a start. Not only did it feel warm to the touch, warm and lingering, but unless it was his imagination, he felt something tickling his palm. A forefinger, perhaps?

'And what do you hope to do in life, Claude?' he enquired.

'We were hoping she would enter a convent,' said Mlle Pichot, 'but at present she is in catering.'

Jet black hair, cut to frame a pale, oval face, might have given Claude an angelic air, but it struck Monsieur Pamplemousse that anyone less likely to entertain thoughts of taking the vows would have been hard to find. It would certainly present a challenge to any Mother Superior who was unlucky enough to draw the short straw. It was tempting to remark that hope sprang eternal from the human breast, but as the girl gave a tiny curtsy, displaying a brief but tantalising glimpse of her unsupported *doudonnes*, he decided against saying any more for fear that his remark might be misconstrued.

'I entered a convent only the other evening,' he said, half jokingly. 'But it was *un accident*.'

It was the second of his comments to misfire. Mlle Pichot fixed him with a beady stare as the girl turned and made her way back down to her place clutching the cup.

'It is not a matter for jesting, *Monsieur*. She is just a simple girl at heart.'

'Aren't they all,' murmured Monsieur Pamplemousse.

Turning to the audience, he decided to play it by ear.

'Rather than bore you with a long speech which in the end may tell you none of the things you wish to know, I thought I would throw it open to you to ask the questions and I will try and provide the answers.'

It seemed like a good idea at the time. He should have known better. Questions weren't slow in coming.

The first was from a girl sitting next to the bespectacled boy he'd spotted earlier. She looked as though *beurre* wouldn't melt in her mouth.

'In the case of the nude brides in the bath, *Monsieur*, were you the first on the scene and was there very much blood?'

He fielded the question as neatly as he could. 'Fortunately, because the murder took place in the bath, blood was not much of a problem. Had it been elsewhere—' He gave the universal shaking of the hand, palm down accompanied by a suitable sound effect.

'So was the plug missing?' It was the same girl again.

'*Oui et non*,' said Monsieur Pamplemousse. 'The young lady was actually sitting on it. That gave me my first clue. What person in their right mind would ever get into a bath and sit on the plug? Clearly, she had been put there by someone, making it a case of murder rather than suicide.'

'My brother sits on the plug,' her spectacled friend piped up. 'He says his girlfriend won't get in with him otherwise.'

'If there was only one bride,' persisted the first questioner, 'what happened to the others and were they all nude?'

Monsieur Pamplemousse took a deep breath. 'They were all in different baths,' he said, 'and yes, they were all nude. People do tend to take their clothes off when they have a bath.'

The ripple of laughter which went round the hall gave him the opportunity to call for the next question.

They followed thick and fast. He disposed of the Axe Murders, then the Blow Torch Victims, followed by the Case of the Broken Bandsaw. During the latter he caught sight of someone standing at the back of the gathering writing furiously in a notebook. That was all he needed – a reporter.

It was time to call it a day. Enough was enough. To renewed cheers from the first few rows he took the easy way out and gave the school the rest of the day off.

Glancing over his shoulder he caught Mlle Pichot's eye. A certain coolness seemed to have set in. Some people were never satisfied.

Postponing the evil moment before the storm broke, he offered to sign autographs before he left and was immediately besieged.

First it was autograph books . . . a few . . . very few. Then it was scraps of paper torn from exercise books, followed by a plaster cast or two. Then someone offered him a felt-tipped pen and a wrist to sign and he made the fatal mistake of obliging. There followed a whole series of wrists; hot wrists, sweaty wrists . . . ice-cold wrists. At the height of it all he became aware of one even warmer than the rest. It had a familiar feel to it, and once again he felt a finger gently tickling his palm, like some Masonic code.

'There is something I wish to ask you, *Monsieur*,' whispered the girl. 'Something I do not quite understand. Perhaps if you have a moment before you leave I could talk with you . . .'

'Oh, Glandier, where are you now?' thought Monsieur Pamplemousse. What was it he always said? 'There's one in every class. Beware of the ones who ask to stay behind because they haven't understood something.' A man of many parts, for a brief period in his life Glandier had been a schoolteacher, but unable to stand the pace, he had resigned before being fired.

He looked at the throng of eager faces surrounding him. With their long, flowing hair, short skirts and hobnailed boots they made him feel old. 'Later, perhaps . . .' he began, 'when things have quietened down.'

All at once he felt the girl give a quick tremor. It happened not once, but several times in quick succession until it felt as though her whole body was starting to vibrate.

She snatched her hand away. 'I must go.'

'Please, do not misunderstand me . . .' For a moment he thought it must be something he'd said.

'No . . . no . . . I will explain later.'

Déjeuner was a muted affair. It might just as well have taken place in the woodshed had it still been there. Mlle Pichot sat at one end of a long table, he sat at the other, and the few staff who had stayed the course occupied the spaces in between. It had all the astringency but none of the after-effects of the Suze he had partaken of earlier in the morning, and as soon as it was decently possible to, he made his excuses and left. At least this time she couldn't run home and tell her mother.

He half expected to find the reporter, if indeed it had been a reporter and not someone writing the whole thing up for the school magazine, waiting for him outside, but he seemed to have disappeared.

Back at the hotel, having first checked to make sure his room had been cleaned and the bed made, he hung the DO NOT DISTURB outside the door, locked it, and let Pommes Frites in through the French windows.

He sat for a moment or two on the leather sofa recovering from his ordeal and trying to account for the strange behaviour of the girl. One thing was for sure, Honoré or no Honoré, he wouldn't be going anywhere near his old school again in a hurry, nor did he expect to be invited. She hadn't mentioned the possibility of another meeting when they said goodbye, so he felt fairly safe on that score. The Director was right. From now on he would be keeping a low profile.

As for Claude, the last he'd seen of her had been as he drove out of the village. She had been talking to someone outside the Hôtel du Commerce. He couldn't be sure, for there was no sign of the dog and the other person had his back to him, but it looked like the man he'd seen trudging through the snow on his way to the hotel the previous afternoon. For a second he had been tempted to stop, but the girl had pointedly looked the other way. Once more he wondered if it was something he had said – or perhaps hadn't said. It was impossible to say. Clearly, she hadn't wished to be seen with him.

The fact that he'd been at Dulac for the best part of a day without even beginning to make a report caused him to reach for *Le Guide*'s case and open it up.

When it was first conceived by the founder,

Monsieur Hippolyte Duval, it had been a comparatively simple affair containing a supply of emergency rations, a tin opener, bandages and a bottle of iodine. Monsieur Duval didn't believe in spoiling himself, although following the invention of the pneumatic bicycle tyre, he had seen fit to add a puncture outfit and a spare inner tube.

It was Monsieur Leclercq who had brought about the greatest changes. First the addition of a pair of Leitz Trinovid binoculars, then a Leica R4 and a selection of lenses so that staff could supply photographic records of their travels. The year before, following an incident when he had been out riding in the Forêt de Fontainbleu and his horse had got a stone in one of its hooves, it had been a top of the range Victorinox Champ Swiss Army knife. And now, with the latest additions: a 650X IBM laptop word processor and a Nikon digital camera, they were ready to enter the twenty-first century.

Reports could be despatched in double quick time via a modem and the nearest telephone line. Only thus, maintained Monsieur Leclercq, could they hope to keep ahead of their rivals. Gastronomy had become a cut-throat business. He could see the day coming when the Director would have route planners installed and Global Positioning so that he could keep track of all the staff. None of them would be safe then.

111

But reports would always have to be filed and edited and entered, and he still preferred the tried and tested method of notepad and pen. At least they didn't require constant recharging. The notebook he kept concealed in the special pocket Doucette had sewn into his right trouser leg was like an old and trusted friend and after switching on the laptop and programming in the appropriate spreadsheet, it was to his notebook he turned first of all before entering in the details.

The orange, raspberry and yoghurt cocktail at the start of his *petit déjeuner* had been a veritable symphony of tastes; a fitting prelude to all that followed: a basket of home-made croissants and brioche fresh from the oven, plates of local ham and cheese – both St-Nectaire and Fourme d'Ambert; another basket containing several types of bread, a dish of *beurre d'Échiré*. A chocolate and cream concoction. The *café* had been accompanied by cold milk as requested. Using *Le Guide*'s system of awarding points for each item, the score steadily mounted until it reached maximum.

He checked the refrigerator. It had been restocked, the glasses replaced; likewise an inspection of the bathroom showed that everything was in order, towels renewed; even the used tablets of soap had been removed and replaced with new ones.

Another reading of the hotel brochure confirmed

his first impressions. Everything seemed to have been thought of. If technical facilities were the prime requirement, Dulac was very definitely Three Stock Pots plus. It was on the cutting edge of scientific progress. State of the art video conference facilities ensured that visitors could be connected to the outside world by means of ISDN fast telephone lines. A 'rollabout' system was available for those who needed to conduct their business from their room. The ISDN system could also compress signals enabling them to be sent by ordinary telephone line. If necessary, sound and pictures could be transmitted globally via satellite. It all sounded very wonderful, but most of it was Greek to him. The Director, always ready to embrace the new, would have been in his element.

Security, too, seemed to have a high priority. An optional extra was video in-car security (ask at the main desk for it to be activated). Any attempt at a break-in and a picture of the intruder would automatically appear on both the television screen in the room and on the hotel's video system. Monsieur Pamplemousse made a mental note to avoid that at all costs. Pommes Frites would not be pleased.

Michelin rated Dulac highly. And no wonder, it was the kind of thing they went for in a big way. He wondered if they, too, had received reports of the recent hiccups. The quote from Gault Millau was the usual tongue in cheek affair, although clearly the gastronomic marriage of classic Auvergne dishes coupled with Japanese cuisine exercised them.

His preliminary work completed, Monsieur Pamplemousse decided to explore the 'Fitness Management Centre', and it was there he discovered where everybody went to during the daytime. It was to the world of keep fit what stationery 'wallets' were to old-fashioned envelopes; everything was on the cutting edge of advanced thinking.

The room was a sea of Bermuda shorts, Spandex and leotards. *Derrières* and bulging thighs loomed large everywhere he looked. People who wouldn't normally dream of mounting a flight of stairs when they could take a lift or an escalator were sweating it out on climbers, treadmills and cycling machines. The air was alive to the sound of whirring pedals, bouncing medicine balls and vibrating stomach belts.

There were ski machines and workout stations of a complexity he'd never even dreamt of: an electromechanical engineer's paradise. All were equipped with automatic pulse control and a polar heart rate transmitter conveying a stream of information to a personal printout device.

A notice on one of the walls said 'Strength Through Joy'. Where had he heard that before? There wasn't much joy on the faces of those taking part. Agony was writ large on many of them. Gold bangles and dangling crosses which, under other circumstances, might well have sparkled, gleamed dully in the overhead lights. Above each machine there was a miniature television camera, relaying a picture to a screen in front of the users. Little wonder most of them had their eyes closed. It was not a pretty sight.

Being temporarily without both a multicoloured sweatband and his Doc Martens and feeling in need of a drink, Monsieur Pamplemousse pretended he'd opened the wrong door, backed away and closed it behind him. He needn't have bothered. Nobody noticed.

It was much the same when he entered the bar. He suddenly felt a foreigner in his own country.

The barman was making a dry martini. It was one up on the Director's favourite method of simply showing the label on a bottle of vermouth to the glass. Having rinsed the inside of a chilled cocktail glass with vermouth, he poured the liquid back into the bottle, filled the glass with gin, then gave a slice of lemon peel a quick twist, skin side down so that the resultant fine spray covered the surface, and dropped it in.

Monsieur Pamplemousse ordered a Suze and turned his attention to the conversation going on around him.

'Hey, take a look at this stemware.'

'Reidel.' The speaker held his glass up to the light.

The newly arrived Americans were discussing their itinerary over champagne. From the conversation it sounded as though they had only landed that morning and yet in their white trainers and loose-fitting Hawaiian shirts they already looked completely at home. He couldn't help but admire their self-confidence. For the second time that morning he found himself feeling overdressed as he tuned in to the snatches of conversation.

'Have you guys worked out where we're headed for tomorrow?'

They were on a gastronomic tour and there were problems with the itinerary. If L'Espérance at Vezeley was closed on Tuesdays and Pic in Valence was closed on Wednesday, how about reversing things and making it Bocuse at Collonges-au-Mont-d'Or outside Lyon and Bernard Loiseau at the Côte d'Or in Saulieu instead? They were both open all the year round.

'Yeah, but will the boss men be there?'

Without wishing to interfere, they had his sympathy. How often had he pored over similar itineraries on behalf of *Le Guide*? Unlike Paris, where most restaurants of note closed for the weekend and that was that, the central parts of France could be the very devil once one got out of synch. At least they were seeing something of the country, which was more than a lot of people staying at Dulac would do. Most would go back home saying they had stayed in the Auvergne and wouldn't even have scratched the surface.

He glanced out of the window. It was starting to snow again. They would be lucky to make any of the restaurants on their list at this rate.

'Monsieur Blanc?'

He gave a start. Conscious of reacting just that split second too late, he looked up to see the Inspector he'd bumped into the previous morning looking down at him. He wondered if all over France his colleagues were having similar problems adjusting themselves to their new code name.

'*Oui.*'

'AKA Pamplemousse, late of the *Sûreté*?'

It was pointless denying the fact and at least it gave him the answer to one of Shinko's cryptic messages.

'Lafarge.' The Inspector held out his hand. 'Mind if I join you?'

Monsieur Pamplemousse hesitated. 'Perhaps over near the window where it will be quieter?'

The Inspector nodded, then stood to one side as a waiter, anticipating the move, took charge of Monsieur Pamplemousse's glass.

'What are you doing these days?'

117

Monsieur Pamplemousse shrugged. 'A bit of this – a bit of that . . .'

'It must pay very well whatever it is if you can afford to stay here.' Inspector Lafarge made himself comfortable with his back to the light.

'*Comme ci comme ça.*' Monsieur Pamplemousse refused to be drawn.

'You have heard the news, of course?' said Lafarge as his drink arrived.

Monsieur Pamplemousse shook his head. 'I have been out all the morning.'

'Ah, *oui*. Of course, the school . . . I hear you have been giving a talk. I trust you will not have given the little ones nightmares?'

'Rather the reverse,' said Monsieur Pamplemousse dryly.

'Time will tell. As it usually does in the end. Tell me, was there much talk in the village of last night's affair?'

Monsieur Pamplemousse shook his head. 'Nothing was mentioned to my knowledge. But since I have no idea what happened . . .'

'*Bon.*' Lafarge seemed pleased. 'We don't want journalists tramping all over the place destroying evidence. At least not for the time being. As to what happened . . .' He gave a shrug. 'It was a case of attempted murder, pure and simple.'

'Murder is never pure,' said Monsieur Pamplemousse, 'and rarely simple.'

'This was a knifing,' said Lafarge. 'It took place outside the *cuisine*.'

Monsieur Pamplemousse gave a whistle. 'I heard a commotion. Cars. Doors slamming. A helicopter at one point.' He paused. 'What was the motive?'

Lafarge gave another shrug. 'Who needs motives these days? They were most likely on the prowl and got disturbed. There were signs of a struggle.'

'You said "they". There was more than one?'

'It could have been a couple of kids. But I doubt it. I have a theory.'

'If I can be of any help . . .'

From the look on Lafarge's face he could tell he had said the wrong thing.

'I think not. The victim is now in a place of safe keeping. He has undergone an operation and is under intensive care. We are waiting for him to come round so that he can make a statement and when that happens I am confident it won't be long before we have it all tied up.'

'So early on?'

'It was not difficult.' The Inspector placed his glass on a nearby table and waved expansively at the outside world. 'The *neige* has given us all the clues we need. A trail of footprints. Fortunately we managed to get photographic evidence before it started coming down again.

'I have never seen anything quite so amateurish. They left their signature everywhere they went. The trail begins at the main gate, leads up to where the crime was committed, then goes all the way back to the main gates again.'

'And then?'

'The footprints disappear in a maze of car tracks.'

'There is no sign of them any further away?'

'I have men looking.'

'Local knowledge is very valuable,' agreed Monsieur Pamplemousse, 'but surely in a hotel with so many people around there must be many such trails.'

Lafarge allowed himself a smile of triumph. 'That is where you are wrong. I already have a very clear picture of the culprits. Finding them shouldn't be difficult.' Clearly he couldn't wait to tell Monsieur Pamplemousse.

'They do say size isn't everything, but in this case it happens to be a crucial factor. Not only are the prints extremely small, they have a very distinctive pattern. I suspect some kind of rubber boots.'

'What the English call a Wellington?' hazarded Monsieur Pamplemousse.

Lafarge ignored the interruption. 'I am looking for two midgets – identical twins most likely, for they appear to be inseparable. One of them had clearly been drinking, for he stopped to relieve himself at the very first tree he encountered. In fact, he could hardly contain himself, for he stopped at a second, then a third. Samples of the surrounding snow have been sent to the laboratory in Lyon for analysis.

'The man's brother, who appears to be the leader, for he was always a few paces ahead, must have the patience of a saint. He always stood to one side and waited.'

'Did he now?'

'It is my theory he didn't totally trust his companion. He never let him out of his sight for a moment.'

Monsieur Pamplemousse gazed long and hard at the Inspector, wondering if he was being serious, then decided he was. It had been a narrow squeak. He had very nearly offered Pommes Frites' services as well as his own. That would have meant a speedy end to their stay.

'It wouldn't be possible, would it, for the whole thing to have happened in reverse?'

'Meaning?'

'Meaning that perhaps the footprints started at the spot where the body was found, went down to the main entrance, then came back again.'

Inspector Lafarge stared at him. 'If that were the case,' he said huffily, 'they would still be somewhere around. Mark my words, I know what I'm talking about.'

'Sherlock Holmes would have been proud of you.'

'*Comment?*'

'He is an English detective,' said Monsieur Pamplemousse. 'A fictional character. He was a past master in the art of building up a picture of a crime from just a few unrelated clues.'

'Was he now?' said Lafarge. 'Well, I'm afraid I have to deal in facts, not fiction. None of your airy-fairy notions.'

Monsieur Pamplemousse hastily changed the subject.

'It is good that you have managed to keep the whole thing quiet so far,' he said. 'Such happenings will not do the reputation of the hotel much good.'

'You can say that again,' said Lafarge gloomily. 'There'll be a few people upset when the news does break. Mark my words.'

Something in his tone of voice made Monsieur Pamplemousse sit up. 'Tell me, who is the victim?'

Lafarge gave him an odd look. 'You mean . . . you do not know? It is Monsieur André Dulac of course. He went outside for a breather after the last of the service and ended up with a steak knife stuck in his ribcage. A *Trappeur* with a 9.5cm serrated-edge blade, for what it's worth.'

Monsieur Pamplemousse knew them well. They used them at La Coupole in Paris. Very effective for their intended task, but hardly a murder weapon.

'Were there any prints?' he asked out of curiosity.

'The handle had been licked clean,' said Inspector Lafarge, 'by an animal, or animals unknown. Nasty. Very nasty.'

Feeling more than ever glad that he hadn't mentioned Pommes Frites, Monsieur Pamplemousse rose to his feet. He was tempted to say that he had to see a man about a dog, but that might have been stretching things a little too.

CHAPTER FIVE

Bathed, shaved and suitably attired for the evening, Monsieur Pamplemousse viewed his reflection in one of the many bathroom mirrors before emerging to face the world. It was too bad he hadn't had time to give much thought to his wardrobe before leaving Paris, but the black roll-top sweater under a lighter shade of bird's eye patterned jacket looked reasonably smart; quite chic in his humble opinion, although Doucette would have pointed out that the jacket was creased in all the wrong places and still smelt strongly of what she had referred to as *eau de Boulogne.*

At least the hotel valet service had turned up trumps with his shoes and trousers; the former as shiny as a new pin, the latter with knife-edge creases that for a change went all the way up instead of stopping short where the top of his trouser press ended.

Sensing an evening of being left to his own devices, Pommes Frites was waiting by the patio door. He was wearing his hard-done-by look, implying that had he been consulted, which of course he hadn't been, he might well have thought up other ways of passing the time instead of sitting in the back of a car, as he suspected might happen. Had life taken a different course, shop stewards might well have been called in to arbitrate; animal rights protesters would have stationed themselves outside the gates.

Having listened to his master's assurances that he wouldn't have long to wait before help arrived, he assumed his slightly pained 'who am I to complain I'm only a dog?' expression, before settling down to await further developments.

All of which struck Monsieur Pamplemousse, who could read Pommes Frites like a book, as being slightly unfair in the circumstances, particularly as he had left the radio on for him. There were times when the complications of human behaviour were hard to explain and *CHIENS* being *INTERDIT* was one of them. It didn't happen very often, but when it did he was usually made to suffer.

He was about to go back inside when he paused for a moment and took a closer look at the door.

Someone had been at it. There were traces of

black powder around the handle. From a distance it could have been the result of someone using a puff of graphite to free a stiff lock, but . . . brushing the surface gently, he held his forefinger up to the light and looked at it . . . on closer examination it clearly wasn't. Whoever was responsible would be in for a surprise if they tried doing the same thing to the car while Pommes Frites was inside it. The thought cheered him up.

Closing the door behind him, he picked up his notebook and slipped it into place ready to start work. Then, conscious that the bulge in his right trouser leg was rather more conspicuous than usual, he removed it. For once it would have to be a case of relying on memory rather than making notes. It was probably better not to be seen writing at table anyway. It was that time of the year when food guides were making their final inspections prior to publication and anyone dining alone was an immediate object of suspicion.

Almost the first person he met as he made his way down the long corridor towards the reception area was Inspector Lafarge. He looked as though he might have been lying in wait for him and his opening words confirmed it.

'I was hoping I might bump into you.'

Monsieur Pamplemousse had been about to say the same thing, but decided to let the other go first.

'*Comment ça va?* Any news of *les minuscules*?'

'You may laugh,' growled Lafarge, 'but I'll tell you something about those two – they're still around. I'd advise you to watch out because they're getting a bit too close to home for comfort.'

'*Comment*?'

'We came across another set of footprints this morning. I'm not sure where they started from, somewhere out near the helicopter pad at a guess, but they led straight to your apartment and back again. We checked the door handle for prints, but all we found were a few smudges.'

'Smudges?' repeated Monsieur Pamplemousse.

'Smudges,' said Lafarge. 'Forensic are still conducting their DNA tests, but I suspect the pair we are looking for will turn out to be itinerant tinkers down on their luck. One of them was probably an unemployed roof tiler. It is a well-known fact in this part of the world that men who work on roofs without wearing gloves wear away the skin on their fingers. It's a common complaint in the trade.

'Tell that to your Monsieur Sherlock Holmes,' he said, barely able to keep the note of triumph from his voice. 'Ask him what he would make of it.'

Monsieur Pamplemousse considered the matter for a moment. He was sorely tempted to take the bull by the horns and suggest it might even be the result of someone touching a hot exhaust pipe, but

Lafarge looked so pleased with himself he had a feeling it wouldn't be appreciated.

'He may have thought they were midgets from a circus who specialise in doing a fire-eating act,' he said at last. 'The handle is unusually high off the ground, doubtless to put it out of the reach of small children. In the case of a pair of midgets one would have needed to stand on the other's back.'

Inspector Lafarge gave him a funny look, as though unsure whether or not to take the idea on board.

'Well, don't say you haven't been warned. If they've been out in the cold all this time they could be getting desperate.'

Bidding the Inspector *bonne soirée*, Monsieur Pamplemousse carried on towards the main reception area where he met the very person he was looking for.

'The same as last night, wuff-wuff-wise?' murmured Shinko as they exchanged greetings.

'I don't think it would meet with any complaints,' said Monsieur Pamplemousse. 'Although a little extra wouldn't go amiss. He is not very happy at being left out of things . . .'

'*D'accord.*'

'You will find him in the car. It is unlocked. I put him in there for the time being in case the room maid came to make up the bed.'

'She's probably done it already,' said Shinko. 'As soon as anyone leaves their room, towels have to be renewed, beds laid out. It'll take a little while to organise you-know-what anyway. Service is in full swing.'

'His boots are in the car too if he needs to go for a walk. You'll find them in the back seat.'

'Brilliant! Leave it to me. I'll let him back into the room as soon as the coast is clear.'

'One other thing . . .'

Shinko looked at him enquiringly.

'Would it be possible to have my car port security system activated?' asked Monsieur Pamplemousse. It struck him that if Lafarge and his men were poking about it might be useful to have any nocturnal visits on record.

'Of course. *Pas de problème*, as they say. It may not be possible until the morning, but leave it with me.' She looked as though she was about to say more, but then she made a face, gave what he'd come to think of as a characteristic wriggle and hurried back the way she had come.

Monsieur Pamplemousse followed her progress across the hallway, wondering what she was really like beneath the black uniform and the laid-back exterior. He shrugged. It took all sorts, and it was nice having friends in the right places.

Pommes Frites' immediate needs taken care of, he

turned his attention to the next important matter.

Looking round the restaurant as he entered he estimated it to be about three-quarters full. Not bad for a February evening in the wilds of the Auvergne.

Unlike some establishments in the remoter parts of France, Dulac stayed open all year round. But it was a chancy business. It was like the theatre. Unless you had at least eighty per cent attendance figures each and every time you opened your doors there was no quicker way of losing money.

In the brief moment while the *maître d'hôtel* came forward to greet him he took stock of his surroundings. The English couple he had seen looking in the *pâtisserie* the day he'd arrived were seated near the door. They must have begun their meal early, for they were already being served *fromage* from a vast chariot. On the far side of the room a waiter took a flash photograph of a table full of Japanese. There was a sprinkling of Germans and Italians. The rest looked as though they were either American or moneyed French; the latter probably in the wine trade.

It was like flipping through the pages of a fashion magazine; a showcase for Hermès scarves, Armani suits, Prada bags, Gucci shoes, Dior gowns, Paloma Picasso costume jewellery, and no doubt later in the evening Platinum Amex cards.

There were out-of-season cut flowers on every

table. Again, as in his room, exquisitely minimalist arrangements in the oriental manner.

Declining the table he was offered, which gave a view of the surrounding countryside, or as much of it as was visible now that night had fallen, he asked for one in the non-smoking area. If there was such a thing at Dulac as a table which was less desirable than the rest, it would most likely be one of the obligatory few reserved for non-smokers. The one he was shown to lived up to expectations, but it suited him well; at least he could remain reasonably anonymous while he watched the comings and goings of the waiters.

The view of the *cuisine* through a long, soundproof window had an almost surreal quality about it. It was like being present while a group of mime actors rehearsed a play without words, although every so often lips moved in response to orders barked out and received. Hands reached up to check order slips pinned above the stations; dishes passed to and fro; the occasional burst of flame cast a flickering glow over the scene as a pan was *flambéed*. There was an air of military discipline and precision about it all, as though if one member were to fall by the wayside another would immediately appear to take his place.

He could see the back of a discreetly placed television monitor adjacent to where Dulac's number two, the *chef de cuisine*, was standing, scrutinising dishes as they left his domain. Glancing up at the ceiling inside the dining area Monsieur Pamplemousse spotted a tiny video camera panning slowly round the room, presumably allowing the chef to make sure none of the guests were kept waiting.

He ordered a glass of the house champagne. An assistant sommelier, a girl, presented the bottle before pouring it. It was Ruinart non-vintage; dry and elegant.

Back in the kitchen area he caught sight of a familiar face. It took him a second or two before he realised it was the girl he had presented the prize to earlier in the day. She looked infinitely more demure in her white overalls, her hair becomingly encapsulated in a matching cap. Honoré hadn't been joking when she said her ex-pupil was in catering. Lucky her. A lot of girls would give their eye teeth for such an apprenticeship. The church's loss was *haute cuisine*'s gain.

Madame Dulac herself was nowhere to be seen. She was probably at her husband's bedside, wherever that might be. The show would go on without either of them, at least for the time being.

He recalled Paul Bocuse's classic response to the question: 'Who cooks when you are away?'

'The same people who cook when I am here!'

That was true up to a point. No *chef patron* of a great restaurant could possibly spend all his time slaving away over a hot stove day in day out. They had a million and one other things to occupy their time, not the least of which was training others in their own style of cuisine, emulating the dishes they had perfected over the years.

Nowadays, too, the world itself had shrunk. Star chefs had become jet-propelled, with invitations to judge a competition here, take charge of the cooking for some great banquet for heads of state there; the demands were never-ending. It needed a strong constitution to stand the pace. Why would anyone want to do it? He certainly wouldn't.

And then again, the public were fickle. They expected to see the Star, if not at work, at least putting in an appearance; making the rounds, shaking hands, wishing the guests *bon appétit*, and all the time smiling as though they hadn't a care in the world. It was the Star the people came to see. His absence was like having a small slip of paper fall out of a theatre programme saying the understudy was playing the leading role.

He wondered how long it would be before word got around. Lafarge was certainly doing his stuff in that respect.

There were two menus. One, the *Menu de Campagne*, was hand-written on deckled-edged parchment and came in a soft leather binding. The other, *Cuisine de Ciel*, a fusion of Eastern and Western styles, freely translated as 'A Marriage Made in Heaven', was presented in a stark white folder. Both bore the ubiquitous letter 'D' on the front; the former in gold foil, the latter in blood red.

While he was studying the first, a plate of *amuse-gueules* was placed before him; tiny portions of *foie gras* in the shape of a duck, the wings fashioned out of finely sliced almonds to cut the richness. They were faultless. So far, so good. It boded well for things to come.

He wished now he *had* brought his notebook with him. It was like being without his Cupillard Rième wristwatch or his favourite Cross pen. His powers of concentration would be tested to the full trying to remember all the details.

He gazed at a photograph of Monsieur Dulac on the inside of the front cover. It was followed by a brief rundown of his career, a kind of CV. Like so many of his generation, François Bise, Bocuse, Chapel, Dulac had done a stint at the Restaurant de la Pyramide in Vienne, first as a commis, then as a *chef de partie*. After that had come a spell under Jacques Pic in Valence, followed by a year at the Grand Véfour in Paris.

From that great fountain of knowledge, Fernand Point, he would have learnt tolerance in a profession not always noted for it, and the need to respect the basic ingredients of his craft, allowing them the freedom to speak for themselves. From Pic he would have learnt generosity. And at the Grand Véfour, under Raymond Oliver's tutelage, he would have learnt to broaden his horizons as a *restaurateur*, enabling him to cater for the likes and dislikes, the fads and fancies, of customers from any walk of life who chose to beat a path to his door.

On his return to Pouligny, Dulac had taken over from his father at the old Hôtel Moderne and in no time at all had come the award of a Stock Pot. The following year he had gained a second and his future was mapped out. The third Stock Pot had been only a matter of time – time and money. The capital investment must have been horrendous; the day to day running costs didn't bear thinking about.

Proof of the latter came only a moment later when the *maître d'hôtel* presented a wicker basket, lifting the lid for inspection. There must have been at least 10,000 francs worth of truffles inside it. The earthy smell helped Monsieur Pamplemousse with his first decision.

Black Périgord truffles were at their best and most flavoursome towards the end of February, when the frosts were over. Consulting the menu again he ordered *truffes sous la cendre* – truffles cooked in the embers.

'It will take three-quarters of an hour, *Monsieur*.'

'I am sure it will be worth the wait.'

'*Ensuite, Monsieur?*'

Monsieur Pamplemousse hesitated. In the normal course of events he would have been expected to comment on at least one of the three specialities recommended in *Le Guide*, but then his visit wasn't exactly normal. Besides, Lafarge had it stuck in his mind that André Dulac's attacker had been someone from outside the hotel. It occurred to Monsieur Pamplemousse that it could just as easily have been someone from inside; possibly even a member of Dulac's own staff. With the underground heating keeping the pathways clear of snow there would be no means of knowing. Tempers flared in the best of kitchens; potentially lethal weapons were to hand. He was no lip-reader, and behind the plate glass window who could tell what was being said? It might be worthwhile testing the system.

'Then . . .' It went slightly against the grain given all the other temptations at his disposal; he ordered an *entrecôte* steak, rare, with *pommes purée* and a green salad.

'*Parfait, Monsieur.*' The *maître d'hôtel* made it sound as though he couldn't have made a wiser choice himself; the best he'd heard that evening.

The sommelier arrived and Monsieur Pamplemousse turned his attention to a voluminous wine list.

Although not unsurprisingly orientated towards nearby Burgundy and the Rhône Valley, it did at least recognise other regions existed, unlike some restaurants he could have named, and it was sufficiently catholic to cater for most tastes and pockets. He happily settled for a Volnay-Santenots-du-Millieu 1991 from Dominic Lafon. His choice received a professional nod of approval followed by the award of a second *parfait*.

The business of ordering disposed of, Monsieur Pamplemousse turned his attention to his fellow diners.

It wasn't all glitz and glitter. At the far end of the room a party of some seven or eight locals were tucking into their food with gusto; gales of laughter punctuated their conversation.

Seated round one of the centre tables were what he took to be four members of a pop group. Despite the low ambient lighting, they were all wearing dark glasses so that they wouldn't be recognised. Not that most of the other diners would have done so anyway.

An American couple entered the restaurant and were shown to a nearby table. The man looked short of breath, as though making the journey from his room to the restaurant had been something of a marathon. His companion, an oversized blonde wearing a dress not only off her shoulder, but off nearly everything else as well, attended to her make-up while he slipped a note to the *maître d'hôtel*, with an injunction to 'look after them'. It was an essay in sleight of hand. They were shown to a table for four by the window. Two place settings were discreetly removed and shortly afterwards a bottle of Krug arrived and was presented.

At another table in the window he spotted the two businessmen he'd seen in reception when he had arrived. His gaze lingered on them. There was a third man present, but he had his back to Monsieur Pamplemousse. Even so, he looked vaguely familiar. And was it his imagination or were they being given slightly less attention than those at the surrounding tables?

The truffle, when it arrived, had been prepared and cooked in the classic Escoffier manner: cleaned, but unpeeled, lightly salted and basted with a little champagne brandy, before being wrapped in a thin slice of fresh pork fat followed by a double piece of buttered waxed paper and then buried in the hot cinders of a charcoal fire. It was served with *beurre d'Échiré*, than which there was no better.

He hadn't expected anything less, but with everyone doing their own thing these days you never knew. It merited all the praise lavished on it over the centuries.

The Volnay was a treat; rich and fragrant, a product of love, knowledge and dedication. Against the snow-white tablecloth the colour was ruby red.

He made a mental note to award extra points to the sommelier for waiting until his glass was nearly empty before refilling it. There was only one thing worse than having an empty glass; that was having it constantly refilled so that you lost track of how much you had drunk and became unable to pace yourself.

Going back to the three men in the window. All three struck a slightly discordant note. Once again he found himself wondering if the first two were bankers. If all the rumours about strange goings-on at Dulac were true they could be getting worried about their investment. He wondered if they knew about the latest attack.

The *entrecôte* steak was unbelievably tender and tasted as though it had been grilled over a bed of vine shoots. Beef marrow must have been added when it was turned, and the criss-cross pattern on the top had been made the old-fashioned way with a hot skewer. A *soupçon* of *Bordelaise* sauce acted as a glaze and it was served with a melting of parsley and shallot butter.

The *pommes purée* were the equal of Robuchon's in Paris, than which there was no higher praise; another lesson, if one were needed, that the simplest dishes cooked to perfection often require the most attention to detail. The potatoes would have been of uniform size, scrubbed and then simmered in salted water to retain the flavour until soft and ready for peeling. Passed through a fine food mill and vigorously stirred with a wooden spoon over a slow heat until dry; only then would chilled unsalted butter have been added, a little at a time, followed by milk brought almost to the boil. After which it would be passed through a fine-meshed drum sieve. The whole thing was so labour intensive it was small wonder only those at the very top of their profession could even contemplate doing it.

The green salad was a simple mixture of dandelion leaves, lamb's lettuce, *radicchio*, served with an equally simple *vinaigrette* made with a blend of virgin olive oil and sunflower oil, with lemon juice to which a little Dijon mustard had been added, rather than vinegar. There was a hint of basil.

The sheer ergonomics of running a three Stock Pot restaurant were mind-boggling. The sourcing of supplies for a start. Not for Dulac any of the tricks of the trade: tomatoes packed while they were still green and given doses of ethylene while *en route* to make them unnaturally red; but always, without fail, the freshest that could possibly be found. The basil was a case in point. Here it was, the middle of winter, and yet he could have sworn the leaves had been freshly picked, torn rather than cut so that they would give off their full flavour.

It was no wonder Guilot had been taken aback at finding a stale lettuce leaf in his salad. As for Loudier's worm: that was something else again.

Monsieur Pamplemousse was left with no regrets whatsoever regarding his own choice, and interestingly, the steak knife was a Laguiole without a serrated edge, which answered his earlier unspoken question.

Resisting the blandishments of the cheese waiter with difficulty – it was the wrong time of the year for many of the local varieties made with cow's milk, and he wasn't prepared to accept the pasteurised factory version – Monsieur Pamplemousse ended up choosing the *bleu d'Auvergne*. It must have been at the end of its curing period, but was none the worse for that. It was served with a small glass of Sauternes.

For *dessert* he had a *tarte fine aux pommes*, the thinly sliced Golden Delicious apples cut into crescents, overlapping each other like petals and moistened with lemon juice. It was served with *crème Chantilly*.

The whole had been as much a marriage made in heaven as anything that might appear on the other menu.

The service had been hard to fault. If he had a criticism it was that, at times, apart from the sommelier, it had been a little too good, slightly manic in fact, with waiters suddenly springing into action for no apparent reason as far as he could see.

Monsieur Pamplemousse dabbed at his lips with the napkin before slowly rising to his feet. It was time to spring into action himself and repair to his room in order to get it all down on the computer before lethargy set in and it was too late.

The American with the blonde already looked as though he might not make it in any sense of the word.

Pommes Frites looked as though he had also dined not wisely, but too well. Tucked up on a spare blanket at the foot of his master's bed, he could barely summon the strength to wag a greeting. A large plate beside him had been licked clean. The shutters were down and his Wellington boots, clean and dry, were by the patio door ready for when he needed them next.

Monsieur Pamplemousse picked up the plate and carried it to the serving trolley which was standing near the door to the corridor. He lifted the domes, half expecting to find a note but there was nothing. Perhaps Pommes Frites had eaten that too? Anyway, Shinko was sticking her neck out on their behalf enough already. Leaving notes for clients would be putting her job on the line if anyone found out.

Feeling strangely lonely, Monsieur Pamplemousse switched on his word processor, called up the appropriate spreadsheet and began entering a few brief notes; key words which he hoped would jog his memory in the morning, rather than complete sentences.

There were over five hundred basic questions on the main sheet, covering practically everything it was possible to think of, but they were mostly of the yes/no variety for feeding into the main computer back at Headquarters where they could be put on file for future reference. It was the individual reports that mattered and required the most thought.

The job completed, he decided to retire early, a task which he performed in rather less time than it had taken him to get ready earlier in the evening.

Reposing on one of the pillows was an arrangement of *véritables praline*; grilled almonds covered in caramelised sugar. Wondering if the room maid or Shinko had been responsible, he tried one before climbing into bed. It had to be from Mazet; the best in all France, as they had been for over three hundred years. The remainder disappeared rapidly. Yet more bonus points for Dulac. He wished him well.

Luxuriating between the soft sheets and the unaccustomed vastness of the space on either side of him, Monsieur Pamplemousse closed his eyes and contemplated his lot. Truly, it had been a memorable meal. A demonstration, if one were needed, of the fact that the simple things in life were often the hardest to get right, but when done to perfection, as they had been that evening, unbeatable.

Apart from that there had been no messages awaiting him in his room. He wondered if he should have rung Doucette. On the other hand the telephone was a two-way thing and if she was staying with her sister she was probably still trying to get a word in edgeways.

There was nothing from the Director. No news of the so-called 'Plan B', whatever that might turn out to be.

As for Dulac, it would have to be a case of wait and see. He would phone through in the morning and report on events so far; the 'accident' in the gymnasium; the business with Monsieur Dulac himself. As for the latter, it would certainly put paid, at least for the time being, to any possibility of the restaurant being awarded a golden lid to its Stock Pots, so in a sense his mission was rendered a bit redundant. And on that unhappy note, Monsieur Pamplemousse fell into a deep, if somewhat troubled sleep.

Pommes Frites heard it first; a tapping from somewhere outside the apartment. He was up and out of the bedroom in a flash. Monsieur Pamplemousse forced himself awake, took a moment or two getting adjusted to the strange geography of the room, then followed on behind.

The sound was coming from the other side of the shutter in the lounge area.

Operating the control button to raise it slowly revealed a figure on the other side of the glass. The light from the room picked out a white face. Silhouetted against the black background beyond, it imparted a strange ghostlike effect.

As soon as the shutter had reached the end of its run Monsieur Pamplemousse unlocked the door and flung it open.

'What on earth are you doing here?'

The girl looked over her shoulder before entering, as though expecting someone else to follow on behind. She wore a leather jacket over a flowered cotton dress. Traces of snow on her black hair were already starting to melt.

'You must be freezing.' Monsieur Pamplemousse took her hand. 'You *are* freezing. Why didn't you come through the hotel?'

'It is late. People would ask questions.'

He glanced at his watch. It showed a little after midnight.

'I wanted to talk to you, but it hasn't been possible. It is about the car.'

'The Twingo?'

'The one standing outside. I haven't been able to

tell you before, but I wonder if it is meant for me?'

Monsieur Pamplemousse stared at her. 'Would you mind saying that again?'

'It is the colour. I was supposed to pick up a yellow Twingo in Roanne two days ago. I went over there specially but something went wrong with the arrangement. I don't know, perhaps it was me. Then, when you turned up here I began to wonder . . .'

'Sit down.' Monsieur Pamplemousse pointed to the settee. 'Let me get you a drink.' He opened the refrigerator. 'A cognac will get the circulation going. Or there is wine . . . champagne if you prefer . . .'

Leaving the girl to help herself, he went to the bathroom in search of a dressing gown. When he returned he found she had poured two glasses of cognac. Pommes Frites was sitting watching her. It was hard to tell what he was thinking.

'I hope you don't mind my coming here like this, but I couldn't think of any other way.' She glanced nervously towards the window.

Monsieur Pamplemousse made for the control panel. 'Would you like me to lower the shutter?'

'No, I think it is better not. I have been wanting to talk to you, but it isn't easy. Especially in this place. There are eyes everywhere.'

'You mean here – in the hotel . . .'

'Everywhere.'

She reached inside the top of her dress and took

147

out a piece of folded paper. 'Here . . . this will explain.'

Monsieur Pamplemousse took the note from her. It felt damp as though she had been perspiring, as well she might have been if she had come any distance through the snow.

As he unfolded the paper she began removing her boots. From the look of them she hadn't come far.

He ran his eyes down the page. It was written on plain, unheaded notepaper and the hand was immediately familiar.

'It isn't from you?' asked the girl.

Monsieur Pamplemousse shook his head while reading the words with growing consternation. It just wasn't possible. And yet, there it was in black and white, or rather white and the particular shade of Royal Blue much favoured by Monsieur Leclercq, who was particular about such things and bought his stationary supplies from Il Papiro in Florence.

'I thought not. I've seen your writing. It isn't like that.'

'When did it arrive?'

'A few days ago. It came by special delivery. That's how I got it. Normally it would have been . . . someone else would have opened it. I do not understand all that it says. About the other things I mean . . . I was hoping you could tell me.'

Monsieur Pamplemousse shook his head. 'I am

as much in the dark as you are. It is all a complete surprise to me.'

'But can you help me? Surely if it is the car and you are driving it you must know where it came from and who it is meant for.'

'That is a natural supposition,' said Monsieur Pamplemousse, 'and it is true I know where it came from. It is also true I was supposed to leave it in Roanne for collection, but . . .'

'In the car park near *le gare*?'

'*Oui*. I was to leave the keys in the exhaust pipe.' He raised his right hand and extended the fingers. 'Unfortunately, it wasn't designed with such things in mind . . .'

'But that is no longer a problem. You have the car, and here am I . . .'

'The problem,' said Monsieur Pamplemousse slowly, 'is that it is not my car and apart from this letter, I have . . . or had . . . no knowledge of who it is meant for. And . . . please forgive me, but I also have no means of knowing for certain that you are that person. I take it you are not carrying your *carte d'identité*?'

The girl shook her head. She looked close to tears. 'Can't you telephone? If only I could talk to someone.'

Monsieur Pamplemousse checked with his watch again. 'It is late,' he said gently. 'There may be difficulties.'

149

Difficulties was putting it mildly. If the contents of the letter was anything to go by he could foresee all manner of possible complications. Monsieur Leclercq might not be best pleased if his wife answered the telephone for a start.

A thought struck him. 'Perhaps if I were to take your photograph? Then tomorrow I could do the same with your *carte d'identité* and we will take it from there.'

While he was talking Monsieur Pamplemousse went to the drawer where he had left *Le Guide*'s case and removed the digital camera from its compartment.

He hadn't had occasion to use it before, but it was no time to be reading the manual and Trigaux in the Art Department had assured him that when it came down to taking pictures, light was rarely a problem.

'All you need is a candle,' he'd said. 'Focus is automatic down to half a metre. Apart from puking on the lens, a babe in arms couldn't go wrong.' Now was the time to put his words to the test. In any case the girl had already removed her leather jacket and was standing in the middle of the room waiting for him.

Monsieur Pamplemousse took up a position opposite her with his back to the window. He pressed the start button and a green light came on. Then he framed a picture in the viewfinder and moved in closer with the intention of taking a head and shoulders close-up. While doing so he became aware of a change in her expression as she put a hand to her mouth and stared wide-eyed in his direction.

'My dear girl. What is wrong? You are trembling like a leaf.' Holding the camera with his left hand, Monsieur Pamplemousse reached for her glass. 'Here, take some more cognac.'

As he held the glass to her lips there was a sudden flash of light. That was all they needed – one of the freak thunderstorms for which the region was renowned. Even so, he was ill-prepared for her reaction.

Her eyes, already wide open, grew wider still. She gave a terrified scream and as her legs gave way, collapsed into his arms.

As though blaming the forces of nature for his master's predicament Pommes Frites ran to the window and began to bark.

Monsieur Pamplemousse, conscious that his world, which only a few minutes before had been one of untroubled peace and tranquillity, was now in a dangerous state of collapse, let go of the camera and dragged the girl in the direction of the sofa, trying to recall as he did so all that he had learnt on his recent course. He particularly remembered the part where they'd had to administer the kiss of life to one of the locals who worked in the orderly office.

To give the girl her due she had given the class full value for their money. It was the one part of the course they had all enjoyed. One or two of the brighter sparks had made a complete hash of it the first time round, and were forced to go through it all over again, some not once, but several times. If there was any justice in the world there was no reason why she shouldn't live to a ripe old age.

As he made to put theory into practice another flash of lightning lit the room.

'*Silence! Asseyez-vous!*' Pommes Frites' barking was enough to waken the dead, let alone the other guests in the hotel. Any moment now someone would be banging on his door.

The possibility spurred Monsieur Pamplemousse on to even greater efforts. There was not a moment to be lost. Ignoring the fact that his dressing gown was rapidly becoming disengaged from the rest of him, oblivious to the renewed flashes of lightning, he gathered the girl in his arms and began work in earnest.

It was as he drew breath before embarking on his fifth – or was it his sixth? – puff of life-giving oxygen, that he became aware of something very strange.

He could feel a vibration coming from the girl. Had he been trying to describe it in a court of law he would have been hard put to find words that would have met with universal approval. Its epicentre appeared to be in her nether regions; that part of her which nice girls were enjoined by their mothers to keep a closely guarded secret until such time as it was right and proper in the eyes of the church to reveal them to a stranger.

Steeling himself to the task in hand, closing his eyes in case she woke while he was in the middle of his investigations, ignoring the renewed flashes of lightning, the frequency of which suggested the storm must be reaching its peak, Monsieur Pamplemousse lifted the girl's dress and embarked on a point to point body search, the thoroughness of which would undoubtedly have stood him in good stead had he been conducting it in Boulogne.

Watching events unfold from his position near the window, Pommes Frites so far forgot himself as to emit a loud howl on his master's behalf.

It was a mixture of commiseration and resignation, overlaid with more than a hint of *déjà vu*. Then, unable to contain himself a moment longer, he hurried across the room to offer his services. Pommes Frites was not the sort of dog ever to desert his master in his hour of need.

CHAPTER SIX

Monsieur Pamplemousse stayed where he was long after the girl had gone on her way. Sleep was out of the question. His mind was racing in a dozen different directions all at once.

Pommes Frites clearly felt the same way. Having seen her safely back to the front of the hotel, he spent the first few minutes pacing to and fro, breaking off every now and then to peer out of the window as though looking for something, or someone. Perhaps he was hoping she would return.

In the end, to put him out of his misery and because, although he wouldn't have admitted the fact to anyone else, he was beginning to feel slightly vulnerable himself, Monsieur Pamplemousse reached for the control button and closed the shutter. As he did so his eyes fell on the pager. It was lying on the sofa where he had left it; a black, plastic object no bigger than a match box, barely 3cm x 2.2cm and perhaps another centimetre thick.

What was the world coming to? Nuns with infrared cameras. Hotel staff with noiseless electronic pagers. Mobile phones were bad enough, but to be constantly at someone's beck and call simply by virtue of being at the receiving end of a vibrator activated by some distant person pressing a button must be purgatory at times. At least with a mobile phone it was possible to respond verbally if need be, or even hang up, or pretend you were stuck in a tunnel. It was no wonder most of the waiters were in a constant state of nervous tension. It also accounted for Shinko's habit of suddenly taking flight for no apparent reason. At certain times of the day, when guests were arriving or departing, she must be in a constant state of flux.

The case still felt warm to the touch and the smell of Jasmine was ever present. For some reason it must have remained jammed in the on position. Cupping it in his hand he could feel a not unpleasant tickling sensation. Perhaps it had overheated. It would be hardly surprising considering where he'd found it. He gave the device a smart tap on the side of the table and it stopped immediately.

He'd eventually located it taped to Claude's body just inside the top of her *culottes*; or rather, to be pedantic, where the top of her culottes would have been had she been wearing any, which patently she wasn't.

To give her the benefit of the doubt she had probably removed them because of the heat of the kitchen, but it was yet another reason, if one were needed, why he felt she should stick to catering as a career. Such dedication deserved to be rewarded and she was definitely not cut out for life in a nunnery.

For no good reason other than the association of ideas, he recalled Doucette once telling him that the pupils at her Catholic girls' school had been made to keep their shoes so highly polished the Mother Superior had been able to check for such things simply by giving them the once over during morning prayers; or so rumour had it at the time.

Pommes Frites joined him, and having sniffed the device with interest, conveyed his findings to that part of his brain which dealt with technical matters, analysed the result, and on receiving the required information gave his master some conspiratorial, not to say worried, looks.

Monsieur Pamplemousse wondered what the range of the pager would be. Once again, it accounted for the girl's strange behaviour at the school prize-giving, but had it been triggered by someone at the hotel or by someone nearer at hand?

As for the Director's letter – and despite the fact

that it was unsigned and the writer had fallen over backwards to avoid betraying his identity, Monsieur Pamplemousse hadn't the slightest doubt in his mind about the authorship – it did put an entirely different complexion on things.

He wished now he hadn't given it back to Claude before she left, but equally he could hardly have kept it. That she was the rightful recipient of the Twingo seemed clear beyond any shadow of doubt; she had been too genuinely wrought-up for it to be anything other than the truth.

Certain phrases in the letter kept coming back to him. '. . . Now that you have successfully attained your *baccalauréat* and have reached an age when, by law, you are able to drive a car, I feel it is only right and proper that your industry should receive its just reward. It will also, I trust, be of assistance to you when you go on to university, wherever that may be . . .' Hardly the letter of a doting father, but then again, it was typical of the Director not to use one word when he could get away with ten.

And as far as he knew, Claude *hadn't* taken her *baccalauréat*. Mlle Pichot would surely have told him if she had. The implication had been that she had left school at the earliest opportunity. Certainly there had been no talk of her going on to university. Unless, of course, the job at Dulac was only a temporary fill-in. And hadn't the girl herself spoken of things she didn't understand? The more questions that came to mind the more confused he became.

Those things apart, it all slotted into place. Hadn't Monsieur Leclercq spoken nostalgically of his trip to the Auvergne all those years ago . . . his first job after he joined *Le Guide*. That would have been at the start of the eighties, which would fit.

It was extraordinary to think that he had managed to keep the matter a closely guarded secret all these years. And in this day and age! But then, in many ways Monsieur Leclercq had an old-fashioned streak to his make-up.

The rest of the letter had been mostly taken up with detailed instructions about where and when to pick up the car in Roanne, all of which Monsieur Pamplemousse knew only too well.

A sudden thought crossed his mind. Before Claude left, and while she was still recovering in an armchair he'd taken a quick shot of her with the digital camera. It would be interesting to see how it had turned out.

Switching on the hotel photocopier, he found the appropriate connecting lead, plugged it into the back of his computer and waited while it was installed. As soon as that had been completed it took only a few moments to unload the image from the camera on to the word processor and once that had been done he found the 'print' symbol with the mouse and pressed the left-hand key. There was a brief pause, then a sheet of paper with a black and white picture began to emerge.

Trigaux was right, it really was child's play. The magic of it all never ceased to amaze him. Scarcely a week went by without some new development appearing in the shops. It was hard to keep pace with it all.

He might have another go in the morning and try for a colour copy, but for the moment black and white would be sufficient for his purpose.

Removing the printout from the machine he held it up to the light and gazed at it long and hard for a while. Then he rummaged inside his case until he found a black felt-tipped pen. A couple of deft strokes on the upper lip, one either side of the nose, did the trick. Placing one hand just below the hairline emphasised it still further. The resemblance to the Director was uncanny. It was a clear case of 'like father, like daughter'.

Monsieur Pamplemousse heaved a sigh of relief. He was beginning to wonder if he had done the right thing in giving the girl Monsieur Leclercq's personal fax number. It had been a spur-of-the-moment decision, but after all, it was ex-directory and there was nothing to connect it with *Le Guide*, or with the Director himself come to that.

All the same, he wouldn't be best pleased if by some mischance a message by someone purporting to be his long-lost daughter got into the wrong hands.

Making a mental note to contact him as soon as it was practicable, but still slightly at a loss as to what to say, and equally unsure as to whether he should risk telephoning him at home or wait until he reached the office, Monsieur Pamplemousse finally retired to bed.

Perhaps there would be no need to say anything. Perhaps . . . although he couldn't see any possible way round it for the moment . . . perhaps in the meantime Monsieur Leclercq himself would have thought up a scheme that would let him off the hook. Time alone would tell.

Monsieur Pamplemousse closed his eyes. Such decisions could wait until the morning. He was a great believer in allowing the subconscious to work things out for him while he slept.

His last waking thought had to do with the man in the restaurant; the one who'd had his back to him. Often the back view of people was more easily recognisable than the front, and he remembered now where he had seen him before. Despite the fact that he was wearing totally different clothes – dressed for the occasion, in fact – it was the same man he had seen trudging up the hill through the snow the day he had arrived at the hotel.

He was woken by the sound of a telephone bell; loud, shrill and insistent. Or rather, what he thought was a telephone bell, but in reality must have been part of a dream, for when he opened his eyes, although there was a red light on the bedside telephone indicating there was a message on the voicemail, all was quiet.

Switching on the reading lamp he reached for his watch. It showed a few minutes past two o'clock; a non-time if ever there was. That was one thing against shutters. It was hard to tell the difference between night and day.

Pommes Frites had no such problems. Opening one bloodshot eye, he checked to make sure all was well, then went straight back to sleep again.

Monsieur Pamplemousse reached across the bed, picked up the receiver and pressed the appropriate button. Shinko's voice came on the line.

'The message from "below stairs" is: "*They* should look in the cemetery." Whoever *they* are. *Dormez bien.*'

She was a past mistress at cryptic messages. As for *dormez bien* . . . He was now so wide awake sleep of any kind was out of the question.

Another thought struck him. Who could possibly have called Claude on her pager while she was in his room? From the way she was dressed she hadn't been on duty. And something fairly major must

162

have put her into a state of shock, causing her to faint clean away. She didn't look the sort of girl who would normally be prone to such things; rather the reverse.

It was a strange twist of fate that she should be working for Dulac. That had to be something else the Director wouldn't have bargained for.

Monsieur Pamplemousse found himself wondering if he even knew she lived in the village. Claude had to be over eighteen if she was old enough to drive a car. Eighteen years was a long time and Monsieur Leclercq must have written many times over the years. And if he didn't know, then how had he communicated in the past? Through a third party? Perhaps via the *poste restante*? That could be it; *poste restante*, to be collected from the PTT in Roanne. There had to be a reason why the Director had suggested a rendezvous in Roanne. He wished now he had seen the envelope, or asked a few more questions. It was also typical of Monsieur Leclercq that he should assume a girl of that age would be able to drive.

Monsieur Pamplemousse set the alarm for 07.30 and turned out the light. These things could wait until morning.

But it was one of those fatal 'I'll just think about one more thing before I go to sleep' nights, when one problem leads inevitably to another, so that by the time he did eventually nod off it seemed only a matter of minutes before he was woken again, this time to a fanfare heralding the early morning high-speed news broadcast.

Breakfast, when it arrived, was every bit as good as the first morning's; or it promised to be, and doubtless would have been had he been allowed to make a start on it. As it was, he barely had time to reach for the butter in order to embark on his first *croissant* of the day when the telephone rang.

'Pamplemousse, for the second time in as many weeks I have hardly slept a wink all night.'

Monsieur Pamplemousse resisted the temptation to say 'that makes two of us'. The Director might ask why, and he wouldn't know where to begin. 'My own night has not been entirely without incident, *Monsieur*,' he said simply.

It was like water off a duck's back.

'Words fail me . . .'

Monsieur Pamplemousse's heart sank. Whenever the Director used that phrase it usually meant quite the opposite. Preparing himself for the worst, he wasn't disappointed.

'Something strange has happened, Aristide. I have received some very peculiar communications via my personal fax machine. Fortunately, because I was unable to sleep I came into the office early, so I was able to intercept them before Véronique arrived, otherwise the poor girl's sensibilities might have been blighted for ever more.

'They are of a most unsavoury nature. I haven't seen anything quite like it since I was last in New York. Coincidentally, that was another occasion when I was unable to sleep. I switched on the television receiver during the early hours and engaged in what I believe is known over there as "channel surfing". I happened to alight on Channel 35. Some of the items left little to the imagination. In one of them there was a housewife doing her vacuum cleaning without so much as a stitch of clothing on. It transpired that her husband was a long distance lorry driver, away for weeks at a time, and she was feeling lonely . . .'

'I have always understood it does get remarkably hot in New York during the summer months, *Monsieur*. People make constant use of the fire hydrants.'

'This was in mid-winter, Pamplemousse. There was three feet of snow on the ground. It was a case of bring your own shovel and she clearly had things other than clearing her front driveway on her mind.'

'You mean the items you have received are of a similar nature, *Monsieur*?' Monsieur Pamplemousse hazarded a guess as to what the Director was leading up to. 'A lot of unsolicited mail comes through on the fax machine these days.'

'They are in like mould,' said the Director grimly, 'but far in advance of anything our American cousins might have dreamt up. They make Channel 35 look like a trailer for *Snow White and the Seven Dwarfs*. Furthermore, they are accompanied by what I can only assume is some kind of threat: "There are plenty more where these came from, so lay off, or else . . ."'

'I have them on the desk in front of me,' continued Monsieur Leclercq. 'A series of photographs the like of which I haven't seen for a long time and trust I never shall again. I haven't been through them all, but funnily enough they are slightly reminiscent of the ones taken of you when you were in Boulogne; the same shadowy figure crouched over his victim, only this time he is wearing a half-opened dressing gown.'

Monsieur Pamplemousse suddenly came awake. It wasn't possible!

'They could be stills taken from an early Hollywood movie where the evil mill owner is about to work his wicked will on one of the hired hands,' continued Monsieur Leclercq. 'The girl in the pictures does indeed bear a strong resemblance to Miss Lillian Gish in one of her more distraught moods, as well she might be seeing her assailant is standing over her, camera at the ready, forcing what looks suspiciously like a large cognac down her throat. Clearly it must have been laced with a noxious substance because the next picture shows her in a state of collapse.'

A large lump of *beurre* fell from Monsieur Pamplemousse's knife and landed on his pyjamas where it lay unregarded.

'*Monsieur*, I do not know where those pictures came from, but . . .'

'No "buts", Pamplemousse. The lack of "buts" is precisely why I am telephoning you. You will find this hard to believe, I know, but I have checked the details on the heading of the paper. The time of origin was 04.53, and the place . . . I trust you are sitting comfortably . . . I have checked the number in *Le Guide*, and the place of origin is Dulac, where you are at this present moment!'

Monsieur Pamplemousse was doing more than sitting comfortably; he was sprawled out in a state of considerable shock. As he struggled to his feet his breakfast tray went flying.

'*Merde!*'

'Pamplemousse! Are you all right?'

'It is nothing, *Monsieur!*'

'I thought I heard the sound of a struggle . . . a cry of "*Merde!*" from somewhere close at hand . . .'

Monsieur Pamplemousse retrieved the napkin and began wiping himself down. '*Monsieur*, would it be possible to fax me a copy?'

The Director sucked in his breath. 'I wonder if that is wise, Aristide. There must be laws covering the transmission of pornographic material. It is one thing to receive such items – especially when, as you rightly say, they were unsolicited. It is another matter entirely to send it. Some of the pictures are much worse than others. *Par exemple*, in the fourth of the series the villain, his eyes closed in ecstasy, has his hand up the young girl's dress.'

'*Monsieur*, I have an even better idea.' Monsieur Pamplemousse clutched at the nearest available straw. 'Why don't you bundle everything together and mail it to me. I will investigate the matter for you at this end . . .' Even to his own ears it sounded a trifle suspect.

'You are a good man, Pamplemousse . . .' said the Director. 'I appreciate your solicitude on my behalf, but . . .' he broke off, and when he next spoke it was in an entirely different tone of voice. Monsieur Pamplemousse's heart sank.

'Pamplemousse, I have in front of me a fifth picture which shows a back view of the perverted miscreant holding aloft an object of some kind. I hesitate to think what it can be. He has been joined by a dog . . . a dog who, even allowing for the degradations of the facsimile system, looks remarkably like Pommes Frites . . .'

Monsieur Pamplemousse took a deep breath. It

was now or never. 'It *is* Pommes Frites, *Monsieur*.'

He held the receiver away from his ear for a moment or two as an explosion at the other end was followed by a stream of verbiage.

'*Pardon, Monsieur . . .*' he broke in at last. 'I repeat, I do not know who sent them to you or who took them in the first place. I most certainly didn't.'

'I can see that,' barked the Director. 'It is patently obvious you were far too busy on your own account.'

'I'm afraid I don't know what you mean, *Monsieur*.'

'You know perfectly well what I mean, Pamplemousse. What is worse, the girl is of an age when she could be your own daughter.'

'Or yours, *Monsieur*,' said Monsieur Pamplemousse dryly.

But Monsieur Leclercq refused to rise to the bait. 'I am glad to be getting through to you at long last, Pamplemousse,' he growled. 'This kind of behaviour is unseemly enough in a twenty-year-old, but in one of your mature years it defies description.

'There is yet another picture of Pommes Frites, clearly taking great delight in egging you on, as seems to be his wont. I don't wonder your colleagues in the *Sûreté* chose to give him to you as a leaving present. His years in the vice squad were clearly not wasted. You are two of a kind.'

'I can explain everything, *Monsieur*. The young lady was cold. She was unsuitably dressed for the inclement weather. I was merely giving her a glass of cognac to warm her up as it were . . .'

'Warm her up for what, Pamplemousse?' asked the Director coldly. 'That is the question.'

Monsieur Pamplemousse let the remark pass. 'I have no idea what caused her to faint. She was having trouble with her vibrator.'

'Her *vibrator*?' repeated the Director.

'It is an electronic device, *Monsieur*. When it is operated it emits a vibration and the girl comes . . . or rather she goes . . . In this particular instance it seemed to have stuck in the "on" position for some reason . . .' Aware of the sound of heavy breathing on the line, Monsieur Pamplemousse allowed his voice to trail away.

'Pamplemousse,' barked the Director, 'I am not entirely naive. I do not live on another planet. I know what a vibrator is.'

'In that case, *Monsieur*, and since the device had stuck in the "on" mode you will understand my position and why the third picture shows me looking for it. I wished to put the poor girl out of her misery.'

'A likely story, Pamplemousse!' barked the Director. 'It is not the construction most readers of *Paris Match* would put on it. The word "groping" springs to mind.'

'Evil is in the eye of the beholder, *Monsieur*,' said Monsieur Pamplemousse virtuously. 'If anyone chooses to think differently I shall simply say I couldn't help myself. I was in love. There was a case only recently. It was in all the *journaux*. The judge was most sympathetic to the poor *homme* who was the subject of the accusation made in the name of Political Correctness.'

'And were you?' barked the Director.

Monsieur Pamplemousse hesitated. It struck him that it might be as well to bear in mind that he was, after all, talking of Monsieur Leclercq's daughter.

'In love, *Monsieur*? Certainly not.'

Monsieur Leclercq gave a deep sigh. 'There are times, Pamplemousse, when you stretch my powers of credulity to the limit.'

'*Monsieur*, I think you are doing the young lady less than justice. At present she is in catering, but there has been talk of her entering a nunnery . . .'

'Not before time!' barked the Director. 'Really, Pamplemousse, you seem to have a fetish for ecclesiastics. Let us hope and pray the *Catholic Herald* doesn't get to hear of it. They will have a field day.'

Cupping the receiver under his chin, Monsieur Pamplemousse removed the butter pat from his pyjama trousers, applied it to a slice of walnut bread, and allowed Monsieur Leclercq's voice to drone on. It had to be someone from inside the hotel. Someone who was able to make use of all the facilities. Furthermore,

171

it had to be someone who knew who he was and where he had come from. Someone who had access to confidential information. Someone who could come and go as they pleased without it being queried.

'I totally fail to understand how you allowed it to happen, Pamplemousse.'

'At the time, *Monsieur*, I took what in retrospect I realise must have been a flash gun for lightning. A passing storm . . .'

For a second or two it sounded as though the Director's office was itself the epicentre of a storm. Monsieur Pamplemousse held the telephone receiver away from his head until it had passed.

He couldn't help thinking that one way and another it had been a very unsatisfactory conversation all round. He hadn't said any of the things he'd planned to say, neither had the Director uttered one word on the subject of the Twingo.

Driving into Pouligny brought one consolation. It had stopped snowing. The sun was out and with it came a change in the atmosphere.

Even Mlle Pichot seemed genuinely pleased to see him when he called in at her office on the off-chance that she might be there.

After a moment's hesitation he revealed the purpose of his visit. 'What can you tell me about the girl, Claude? The one I presented the prize to.'

'Why do you ask?'

'I have my reasons.'

'She is no longer my responsibility . . .' Mlle Pichot gave a shrug. 'What is it you wish to know?'

'I am interested in her family background. Where she is from. That kind of thing. It is all perfectly honourable, I assure you.'

'She is not in trouble?'

'Rather the reverse. I may have some good news for her.'

'Do you not know?'

'Should I?'

'I can only suggest you take a walk through the *cimetière*. It is all there, written in stone.'

'It is the second time this morning I have been told that.'

Mlle Pichot gave another shrug. 'Pouligny is a small village. There are few secrets, except perhaps from those who are most concerned. If you do nothing else you could perhaps be instrumental in righting a few wrongs.'

'Is it possible . . . may I suggest we make up over another Suze?'

This time it was Mlle Pichot who hesitated. 'Why not? Life is too short to quarrel.'

Some thirty minutes later, armed with the information Honoré Pichot had given him and fortified by the Suze, Monsieur Pamplemousse made straight for the cemetery. He pushed open the wrought-iron gates in the high stone surrounding wall and went inside. Despite the weather there were a few tracks in the snow where others had been there before him to place flowers or pay their respects to the dead. Otherwise, not surprisingly, it was deserted.

He came across the Dulac family grave almost at once. It would have been hard to miss it. Relatively new and well cared for, it occupied a place in what must at one time have been a central path. Sheltered from the weather by a wall on three sides and a glass roof, protected in front by an iron grille, it was there for all to see and admire. Beyond it stood a group of stone urns filled with artificial flowers. Beside each of them lay a book carved out of white marble, all with an appropriate text in memory of various relatives down through the ages. Some had a simple head and shoulders reproduction of a likeness set in an oval frame; others a more elaborate scene showing a person going about their daily task. Along the back wall, to either side of a central display of flowers taller than the rest, inlaid in gold on black marble, there was a list of names and dates.

Monsieur Pamplemousse took out his notebook and while Pommes Frites waited patiently by his side began with Prosper Dulac . . . Born 1864 died 1929.

Then came Gaston, born 1904 died 1975. André had been born in 1948.

After he had finished with the Dulac family grave he made his way on down the path to a war memorial at the back of the cemetery and stood for a moment or two in silence as he read the names. As always a feeling of sadness came over him. There was the inevitable list of all those who had fallen at an early age during the carnage of the First World War. Many of them he remembered from stories he had been told as a boy. Beneath it there was a smaller list of those who had given their lives in the Second World War. The names were all too familiar.

After France was overrun, a million-and-a-half French soldiers had been packed off to Germany. Ostensibly as prisoners, but in reality to work as slave labour. Hardly a family in the occupied zone had remained unaffected. His own family had lost a favourite member: Uncle Didier, who by an unhappy twist of fate had made his home on the wrong side of the makeshift border just prior to the war. He, too, went off and was never heard of again.

Then, on 11th November 1942, following the Allied successes in North Africa, the Wehrmacht had crossed the demarcation line dividing the occupied zone from the so-called free zone, the Vichy area, where he'd been born and brought up, and it had been the turn of the South.

It was then, fearing for their son's life and believing that it was easier to stay clear of the authorities in the big city than it was in the country where everyone knew what was going on, his parents had packed him off to Paris to live with his aunt Hortense, and his childhood, such as it had been, had come to an end.

Alongside the main memorial there was a tiny patio devoted to those who had died as members of the Resistance. The wall at the back had small blocks of white stone let into it at intervals, each with the name of a person who had been killed, and in the centre there was a simple stone bench which someone had swept clear of snow.

Most of the blocks bore a date in June 1944 when 3000 men from the Underground Movement, having assembled at a point south of Pouillac, held the German Army at bay for several days. It happened after he had left the area, but he remembered hearing about it at the time and afterwards reading about it. Revenge had been swift and bloody – twenty-seven civilians massacred in cold blood. Running his eye along the stones Monsieur Pamplemousse saw the name Dulac carved on one of them. He compared it with his list. It was from what he had come to think of as the main branch of the family. According to Honoré the other side had not exactly been unwelcoming to the occupying forces. Perhaps the episode had been another turning of the knife in the wound.

The second family grave was where Honoré had said it would be, tucked away in a little used corner of the cemetery and open to the elements. Ill-tended. The name Claude went all the way through.

At one point while his master was busy writing Pommes Frites pricked up his ears. His skill as a sniffer dog was never in any doubt, but he was also possessed of an acute sense of hearing. What to most people might have been the simple crunching of footsteps in the snow, not dissimilar to the sound of cotton wool being torn apart and equally innocuous, was immediately recognisable and identifiable.

It was just such a sound that had caught his attention, but since it was receding rather than coming closer, and since his master had just snapped his notebook shut, indicating it was time they were on their way, he chose to ignore it.

Back in the hotel room the red light indicating there was a message on the voicemail was flashing. Ignoring it for the time being, Monsieur Pamplemousse rang Room Service and ordered lunch. Apart from anything else, it was high time he and Pommes Frites had a get-together over a meal.

It turned out there were three messages for him.

The first was from Doucette wishing him

a happy Valentine's Day and wondering if all was well since she hadn't heard. Black mark Pamplemousse!

The second was from Shinko. 'Sorry about the security system outside your room. I had it switched on after I saw you last night and for some strange reason a person or persons unknown deactivated it. Let me know what you would like me to do.'

Monsieur Pamplemousse replaced the telephone receiver and stood staring at it for a moment or two. It had crossed his mind to wonder why the alarm hadn't gone off the night before, but he'd assumed Shinko hadn't been able to oblige.

If someone had switched it off deliberately, then two could play at that game.

He picked up the phone, dialled the Paris code, and rang Trigaux on his direct line. He answered on the second ring.

Pleasantries disposed of, Monsieur Pamplemousse dived straight in. 'Strictly between ourselves, I have a bit of a problem.'

'So what's new?'

'I'm not sure if you can help. It's a bit technical . . . to do with security . . .'

His ploy worked. Trigaux rose to the bait beautifully. In keeping with *Le Guide* going digital he had become something of a boffin on the subject of security in general and computerised information techniques in particular. He was only too keen to air his knowledge, although there were times when he could have been speaking a different language. 'Buzz words' was one of his favourite phrases. Life became more complicated by the minute. Even making a telephone call was no longer simply a matter of dialling a number; according to Trigaux it involved GSM, the global system for Mobile Communication, with bits and bytes, and words like encryption, algorithms and data compression thrown in for good measure.

Monsieur Pamplemousse heard the sound of information being typed in while he was talking.

'Is that all?' asked Trigaux when he had finished.

'It is possible?'

'With all the facilities you have at your disposal you could send a picture to the moon if you wanted to.'

'How about Paris?' It occurred to him that the less he involved the hotel's own security system the better.

'Paris? *Pas de problème.* I could even get it plugged through to Monsieur Leclercq's home in Fontainbleau if need be.'

'You could?'

'You know what a sucker he is for having all the latest gadgets. "We must do everything possible,

Trigaux, to make sure *Le Guide* is brought up to speed and on to the loop.'" Trigaux did a passable imitation of Monsieur Leclercq in full flight.

Monsieur Pamplemousse hoped the Director wasn't within earshot.

'Leave it with me. I'll come back to you on that. I'll just have to check a few things first.'

Déjeuner arrived just as Monsieur Pamplemousse was about to listen to the third message and there was barely time to usher Pommes Frites into the bedroom before he heard the sound of an entry card operating the lock and a ubiquitous trolley with a bevy of polished domes nosed its way in.

A chilled bottle of '93 Leflaive Puligny Montrachet opened, tasted and approved, the bill signed and the waiter safely on his way, Monsieur Pamplemousse disposed rapidly of some *amuse-gueules* – tiny *gougères* of *choux* pastry filled with a mixture of Gruyère and Parmesan cheese. He was on his last one by the time Pommes Frites rejoined him.

Tucking one corner of a large white napkin inside his collar, he refilled the glass and set to work on a bowl of *soupe aux écrevisses de rivière*, a dish of such an exquisite delicacy of taste it almost defied analysis. It would have been tempting to report it as a magical experience, but magic had nothing to with it; an infinite attention to detail would be nearer the truth. Underlying the dominant flavour of crayfish, he detected onion, tomato, carrot to give it body, tarragon, and what must have been a *bouquet garni* of other herbs. There was a hint of garlic, too; armagnac and cream had been added, possibly port wine. In the interest of continuing his researches, he would happily have called for another bowl and made that his complete meal. It had been a delight to all the senses.

On the other hand, such dilly-dallying wouldn't have gone down at all well with Pommes Frites. Pommes Frites wasn't deeply into *amuse-gueules*. In his opinion they were usually so small they constituted a complete waste of time. Nor was he particularly enamoured of *soupe aux écrevisses de rivière*. A couple of good laps and it was gone. He much preferred diving straight in to the *viandes* section of the menu; in this instance a vast plate of local *charcuterie*: ham, both raw and baked in pastry with Madeira, cold meats of various kinds, liver sausage, several generous slices of pork liver *pâté* and a selection of home-made *boudin*.

Monsieur Pamplemousse left him to it while he helped himself to some cheese from another plate. By the time he had taken the first bite from a slice of *Fourme de Cantal*, once again at the end of its curing period, but clearly from a local farm and beautifully kept, Pommes Frites had licked his plate clean and had his eyes on a plate of assorted *tartelettes*.

Monsieur Pamplemousse pretended not to have noticed.

Of the three – *orange, pruneaux* and *citron* – he decided he liked the *citron* best and he was glad he had left it until last. It cut through the sweetness of the first two and prepared his taste buds for the bowl of deliciously plain yoghurt.

By the time he had finished, a response from Trigaux was coming through on the fax machine. Having spent most of his life in the dark, approachable only when the red warning light outside his darkroom was off, coming out into the open seemed to have given him a new lease of life. He liked nothing better than to be faced with a problem he could get his teeth into and he had certainly gone to town on this one. There were eight pages in all, including a long list of requirements and a hand-drawn schematic diagram of the necessary connections for a hook-up.

Seeing the voicemail indicator still blinking reminded Monsieur Pamplemousse that he hadn't listened to the third message.

It was the Director. 'This is terrible news, Aristide. I have just heard it on the car radio. Doubtless you will bring me up to speed as soon as possible. In the meantime . . .'

He could hear Véronique's voice in the background and the sound of two more telephones ringing. He never did catch the end of the Director's message.

Calling reception, Monsieur Pamplemousse asked if he could possibly speak to Shinko. Luck was with him. He was put through almost straight away.

'Can you talk?'

'Sort of . . .'

'I suggest you leave the security alarm for the time being.'

'*D'accord*. Let me know if you change your mind.'

'I hear the news is not good.'

'Worse than not good. Doomsville.' It sounded as though she had her hand over the mouthpiece. 'Someone got into the hospital during the night and put a bullet into *you know who*.'

On the spur of the moment he asked a question which had been on his mind.

'You don't have a camera I could borrow, do you?'

'Me? You must be joking. I'll see what I can do for you if you like.'

Monsieur Pamplemousse thanked her, declined the offer and rang off.

He wondered if he should try phoning the

Director back, then decided against it. There was nothing he could say for the time being. Instead, he picked up the pile of faxes, skimmed through them again, then signalled Pommes Frites to make ready.

Clearly a visit to the local *bricolage* was high on the agenda, and the way things were going the sooner they took off the better.

CHAPTER SEVEN

'Pamplemousse, I cannot tell you what a stroke of good fortune this is. It couldn't have happened at a more opportune moment. I think it is safe to say that Michelin have nothing remotely like it in their pipelines.

'I trust you will let this go no further, but without revealing any names, Chantal and I are entertaining some highly placed members of the upper echelons of government this evening. A summit meeting of heads of state is scheduled to take place in France in two months' time and my advice has been sought as to a suitable venue.'

Monsieur Pamplemousse could picture the scene. The Director's house, situated as it was on the edge of a tranquil forest glade some 30km south-west of Paris, was ideally placed for high-powered discussions of a confidential nature. Indeed, had it been any larger it would have made an ideal *rendezvous* for the summit meeting itself.

No doubt the hedges surrounding the equally tranquil gardens would be given a final tonsorial going-over that afternoon to ensure they would be standing to attention when the guests arrived.

The Director was in his element on such occasions. He loved doing things in style. Monsieur and Madame Leclercq were the only people he knew who had their table laid with antique Sèvres plates solely for show. As in many of the grander three Stock Pot restaurants, where using them as even a temporary depository for the odd olive stone was considered bad form, they were removed before the food arrived lest their delicate surface be damaged in any way.

'I suggested the Hôtel Dulac some weeks ago,' continued the Director, 'because it meets all the stringent requirements. It is remotely situated. It has a helicopter landing pad. The cuisine is, or was until recently, of the highest order, the service and attention to detail beyond reproach, and I trust you will solve that little problem in the not too distant future. Above all, there is their unparalleled investment in matters relating to security. Your latest efforts in that direction are the icing on the cake as it were and I hope will set the seal on the case I have put forward.'

'It is only an experiment, *Monsieur*,' said Monsieur Pamplemousse nervously. 'A spur of the moment idea . . .'

'Spur of the moment ideas are at the very heart of progress,' boomed the Director. 'Trigaux assures me there is no technical reason why the test shouldn't go ahead successfully. As for the untimely demise of Dulac, it is, of course, an unforeseen setback, but if all I hear is true and the perpetrators of the crime are merely two dropouts, not only socially disadvantaged, but physically as well, there will be no slur attached . . .'

Monsieur Pamplemousse listened with only half an ear. The Director was, in any case, his own best audience and there were times when he needed no other.

It was no wonder Lafarge was anxious to get the case tied up as quickly as possible. Having a summit meeting take place on his territory would be a big feather in his cap. The Director, too, would be able to bask in the reflected glory should his advice be taken. As for his talk of killing two *oiseaux* with one stone . . . three *oiseaux* would be more like it. For all Monsieur Pamplemousse knew there might be other fledglings just around the corner waiting to leave the nest.

'And the Twingo, *Monsieur*?' he broke in. 'What are your plans for that?'

Monsieur Leclercq dismissed the interruption with a metaphorical wave of his hand, much as one might brush away an errant fly. Clearly, it was a case of one problem at a time.

'I am doing what I should have done in the first place, Aristide. I am making arrangements with a Renault agency in Roanne. There is one in the avenue Gambetta near the *gare*. You can drop it off there when you have concluded your investigations. Afterwards you and Pommes Frites can complete the journey by train.

'In the meantime I will send a letter of authority to the appropriate person. As for the Hôtel Dulac, in accordance with our normal policy we will leave the allocation of Stock Pots blank for a year and take it from there. As ever, there will an inevitable drop in trade, but if they do play host to an international conference the publicity will be enormous and it will soon pick up again.

'Now I suggest we synchronise watches. *Dîner* this evening is 19.30 for 20.00. Allowing time for *apéritifs*, we are scheduled to be seated by 20.30. The ideal time for your demonstration will be after the first course – we are having *Feuilleté de Saint-Jacques aux truffes* – so, shall we say 21.00? That is four hours, thirteen minutes from now.'

Monsieur Pamplemousse went through the motions of synchronising his Cupillard Rième watch with the Director's. He made it only four hours twelve minutes, but anything to keep him happy. Then, with the final injunction: 'Remember, Pamplemousse, we are merely making use of the technology which exists to connect those who are in need of information with those who have it in their power to provide it. It is as simple as that . . .' ringing in his ears, he replaced the receiver and surveyed the tangle of cables on the floor.

It was all very well for the Director to talk. He didn't have to do any of the connecting.

Picking up the sub-miniature video camera he had removed from the parking area outside, a Toshiba with a wide-angle lens and a light sensitivity down to 0.04 lux, whatever that might mean (according to Trigaux, it was more than adequate for the job in hand), he tried attaching it to one of the dog harnesses he had purchased in the village. It had seemed like a good idea at the time, but he was beginning to have his doubts.

Pommes Frites eyed his master equally dubiously as he began putting two and two together. First there had been all the measuring he had undergone in the shop, now this . . .

Not since he'd been on his induction course had he worn a harness, and the one his master was working on at that moment was like nothing he had ever seen before. It was more akin to the kind of jacket he'd occasionally seen being used to calm people down when they were taken in for questioning and didn't want to go.

Searching through the thirty-one different features contained within the Victorinox Swiss Army knife, rejecting one by one such things as the corkscrew, the tiny wood saw and an equally small wood chisel, Monsieur Pamplemousse found the tools he thought looked most suitable for the task in hand and set to work, musing as he did so that there were times in life when everything seemed preordained. Who would have thought, *par exemple*, that the simple fact of the Director's horse getting a stone in one of its hooves would come in useful so many years later.

Rabillier, who ran the stores and was responsible for ordering a supply of the knives in the first place, always maintained it had been a bit of equine subterfuge on the horse's part; a mute protest over the Director's increasing weight. But like many in his calling he had become more and more of a cynic over the years and viewed the world beyond his counter with a jaundiced eye. Glandier maintained the day would come when he wouldn't hand over anything at all to anyone.

Monsieur Pamplemousse wasn't sure which feature proved the most useful in the end; the fine screwdriver, the awl, the toothpick, the magnifying glass, or the fish scaler with its hook disgorger; but in combination they did the job admirably.

Reflecting on a job well done, he doubted if even in his wildest dreams, Karl Elsener, perfectionist that he was, could have pictured back in 1891 that one day his invention would become the gift of presidents, *de rigueur* aboard NASA's *Columbia* space shuttle, and prove a godsend, not just to officers in the Swiss Army, but to people in all walks of life, from students to farmers, from lumberjacks to climbers, and from fishermen to food inspectors wishing to attach a small device to the top of a bloodhound's head so that pictures could be transmitted over vast distances, even to the moon and back if the need arose. He wouldn't have believed it himself not so long ago.

Had he been able to find the tiny ballpoint pen which was in there somewhere, he would have sat down and written a letter of thanks to Monsieur Elsener's successors.

In the main, the booklet which accompanied every knife happily confined itself to illustrating such humdrum tasks as the peeling of apples and the straightening of ladies' eyelashes. But for anyone who felt the need to attach a miniature video camera and its associated equipment to a dog, it was ideal.

It was a testament to the hardness of the chrome

molybdenum stainless steel awl that it managed to penetrate a piece of old leather so hard and so misshapen it was impossible to tell what its original purpose had been, if indeed it ever had one. Having first applied a plaster to a surface wound on his right knee, which had been briefly pierced at the same time, Monsieur Pamplemousse set about carrying out some running repairs to his fingernails with the aid of the scissors and a file.

Pommes Frites, for his part, was beginning to look less and less enthusiastic about the whole thing. After his master had finished attaching everything to him, he shook himself several times, and when that didn't work, he attempted to dislodge it all by the simple expedient of arching his back and crawling under the table until he got himself stuck.

Leaving him where he was for a moment or two in the hope that he would become accustomed to his new role, Monsieur Pamplemousse switched on the nearest television receiver, applied power to the camera and the transmitter module, then ran through the channels until he found the right one.

Pommes Frites' eyes grew large as a picture unfolded itself on the screen, rolled over once or twice, went white all over, then quickly darkened as the camera automatically adjusted itself to the ambient light in the room.

A series of thuds caused by a tail making contact

with the underside of a glass tabletop signalled his seal of approval as the television settled down to reveal the face of his master looking down at him.

Monsieur Pamplemousse breathed a sigh of relief. He picked up the telephone receiver and dialled Trigaux's number. So far, so good. He had cleared the first and potentially most problematic hurdle. From now on he was content to let others take over.

For the first time since he had arrived in Pouligny Monsieur Pamplemousse was actually enjoying himself.

Trigaux summed it all up in one word – *parfait*! An hour and a half had passed since Monsieur Pamplemousse first called him to say that everything was all right at his end and now, the final link having been established via the World Space Digital Broadcasting System, everything was in its place and working.

The Director was fulsome in his praise and positively oozing satisfaction. 'At the risk of being boring, Pamplemousse,' he boomed, 'I say again, this couldn't have happened at a more opportune moment. If everything goes according to plan it will be a signal honour for us all.'

Such was Monsieur Pamplemousse's own state of euphoria he hadn't even noticed Monsieur Leclercq repeating himself. All the gossip he'd heard since he had arrived at the Hôtel Dulac, much of it exaggerated no doubt, but serious none the less; talk of itching powder finding its way into the air-conditioning system, and *alors!* the time when a dead rat had been found in the main drinking water tank, paled into insignificance.

Seeing pictures appear on the television in his room as Pommes Frites, the camera perched on his head, set off on his rounds, made even the murder of Monsieur Dulac seem like yesterday's news. It was akin to the never-to-be-forgotten moment when, as a small boy, electricity had first been installed in his parents' home. For days afterwards the simple act of switching the light on and off had been a magical experience.

As for Pommes Frites, he was positively revelling in his new role of roving investigative reporter, although in the nature of things he missed the best bits because each time he rushed back to the hotel to see what was happening on the television he registered surprise because it still showed the inside of the room. Monsieur Pamplemousse tried recording a section in the hope that he might connect cause with effect, but it still didn't work. In his own simple way, seeing the look of pleasure on his master's face was, in itself, sufficient reward. The frequent pats on the head, icing on the cake.

Pommes Frites' explorations took the shape of ever-widening circles. First there was the copse. Then he ventured as far as the main gates. That was followed by the helicopter landing pad, fortunately deserted, then he took in the dining room. Anyone happening to glance out of the window and seeing him go past might well have had second thoughts about the wine.

It occurred to Monsieur Pamplemousse that Inspector Lafarge would have a field day in the morning when he saw all the trails running hither and thither. It would be interesting to hear his theories.

He waited five minutes until his watch said 20.55 before sending Pommes Frites off on his first serious patrol. The sky was clear, and with the moon approaching its zenith, conditions couldn't have been better. The picture he was receiving in his room was quite extraordinarily clear. Better, in fact, than if he had been there in person. He heard a round of applause over the telephone line. It was accompanied by the sound of clinking glasses and cries of *'Bravo! Bravo!'*

'Excellent, Aristide. Excellent.' The Director's voice sounded muffled. He either had his hand over the telephone receiver or he had fallen behind with the *Feuilleté de Saint-Jacques*. Monsieur Pamplemousse strongly suspected the latter. He looked at his watch. The galling part about the whole thing, of course, was that once again as far as he was concerned it might well turn out to be a case of eating in his room. There would be no great call for the toothpick attachment to his Victorinox knife.

'This is most exciting,' continued the Director. 'Not dissimilar I imagine to the moment when a Frenchman first discovered television.'

'With respect, *Monsieur*,' Monsieur Pamplemousse found himself whispering along with him, 'I think it was a Scotsman. A Monsieur Baird.'

'Ssh!' hissed the Director. 'We must not upset Monsieur le Ministre. He is very sensitive on these matters. Just for tonight, please try and remember it was a Frenchman.'

Before Monsieur Pamplemousse had a chance to say any more his attention was drawn by a change of picture on the television screen. Perhaps sensing the importance of the occasion, Pommes Frites seemed to be taking a different course this time; one which took him over somewhat rougher terrain. Every now and then the camera did a quick 180 degree whip pan. Clearly, he was taking stock of the situation, looking over his shoulder to make absolutely certain no one was following him. Turning up the volume control revealed the sound of heavy breathing.

'He appears to be in pursuit of someone . . .' The

Director, his voice pitched low as though from fear of being overheard, echoed Monsieur Pamplemousse's own thoughts.

He made a mental note to tighten the harness. The camera mounting must have slipped. It was now showing more of Pommes Frites' head than it had before. The horizon, which had been near the top of the frame a few moments earlier as he moved forward with his head to the ground, was now almost level with the bottom. The moon appeared momentarily in the top right hand corner and there were occasional glimpses of twinkling lights, not unlike the star effects in a television spectacular.

It didn't appear to be troubling Pommes Frites because at one point he looked round and if Monsieur Pamplemousse hadn't known him better he could have sworn he was smiling. Doubtless it was distortion due to the proximity of his face to the wide angle lens.

The sight elicited a stifled cry of alarm from the Director. 'Pamplemousse,' he hissed, 'what *is* going on?'

Monsieur Pamplemousse hastened to pour oil on troubled waters. 'I think he is having trouble with his straps, *Monsieur*. The device is, of course, merely a prototype. I can already see possible improvements for the Mark II.'

'If Pommes Frites continues gloating in that

singularly unpleasant way,' hissed the Director, 'there won't be a Mark II. Is there nothing you can do to stop him? And another thing. I have just been asked a very pertinent question by Monsieur le Ministre. It is simply this: Why is Pommes Frites making such slow progress? The horizon has been going up and down now for several minutes, but it seems to be getting no nearer.'

'I think possibly he is caught in a snowdrift, *Monsieur*.'

'Be that as it may, Pamplemousse,' Monsieur Leclercq sounded dubious, 'but is it not possible to zoom out so that we can see more of the immediate lie of the land? I understand from Monsieur le Ministre that the technical term has to do with establishing *"le geographié"*. Also, while you are doing that would you please see if you can adjust the sound. The constant heavy breathing sounds like an obscene telephone caller of the very worst kind. It is putting the Monsieur le Ministre's wife off her *dîner*. She is finding it difficult to do justice to the *cuisson*.'

Monsieur Pamplemousse felt like saying *baiser* Monsieur le Ministre and his *femme*, particularly his *femme*. At her age she ought to consider herself lucky. Some people were never satisfied. He recalled the time when Glandier had had a remotely operated garage door installed and for weeks afterwards colleagues had been invited round to dinner for the express purpose of seeing it work. Then one day when he was late for work he got so impatient with the slowness of it all he endeavoured to anticipate things. Forgetting his aerial was raised, he got it entangled with one of the overhead wires and it brought the whole lot crashing down on top of his car roof. Madame Grante's damage report had taken him several days to fill in.

Having counted up to *dix*, he was about to launch into a dissertation on the technical differences between a fixed focus and a zoom lens and the impossibility of carrying out the Director's request with the former, when matters resolved themselves in no uncertain manner.

The horizon suddenly swam into its correct position about two-thirds up from the bottom of the frame and as the picture righted itself electronics took over. Automatically balancing the contrast between the darkness of the principal subject and the whiteness of the snow, as Pommes Frites detached himself, it revealed in sharp focus what was undeniably the rear end of a large black dog.

At the same time a shadowy figure entered the frame left uttering a cry of *'Asseyez-vous! Asseyez-vous!'*

Almost immediately the dog set off at high speed. A split second later Pommes Frites sprang into

199

action. The effect was rather like that of an express train entering a tunnel as he followed on in hot pursuit.

Monsieur Pamplemousse stared at the scene, conscious as he did so that others all the way along the line were doubtless reacting in their different ways.

He hadn't long to wait before the Director gave voice to his feelings.

'Are you there, Pamplemousse?'

For a split second and out of a sense of self-preservation, Monsieur Pamplemousse toyed with the idea of saying *non*, but logic came to his rescue.

'*Oui, Monsieur.*'

'Did you see that?' barked Monsieur Leclercq.

'*Oui, Monsieur.*' Having agreed to the first question he could hardly deny the second.

'Pommes Frites is up to his old tricks again! Like master like hound. Really, if the atmosphere is being polluted by constant exposure to the transmission of such images, it is little wonder the world is becoming such a sorry place. Exhaust fumes from automobiles are the least of its problems. There is only one word for it and that word, Pamplemousse, is *débâcle*! We will discuss this whole matter in the morning.'

'*Oui, Monsieur,*' said Monsieur Pamplemousse

meekly. *'Bon appétit, Monsieur.'* He nearly added *dormez bien*, but by the sound of it he doubted if Monsieur Leclercq would be getting much in the way of sleep that night.

He had hardly replaced the receiver when the phone rang again. 'Hard luck,' said Trigaux. 'You've got to hand it to Pommes Frites. He doesn't miss a trick.'

That was another way of putting it.

By the time he had finished with the telephone calls the screen had gone blank, possibly because the batteries were flat, but Monsieur Pamplemousse was past caring.

He switched the television receiver off and with a distinct lack of enthusiasm set about dismantling the hook-up in his room. No doubt Pommes Frites would return from his wanderings in his own good time and there was no point in crying over spilt milk. Nor would there been any point in scolding him when he did get back for something which by then would be relegated to the past. Like most members of his species Pommes Frites lived for the moment, seizing opportunities as and when they came his way. He had only been obeying his natural instincts and memorabilia didn't play a large part in his scheme of things.

Monsieur Pamplemousse's reveries were broken into by a shuffling noise coming from somewhere outside, rather as though a heavy object were being dragged along the path. Returning the video recorder to its rightful home, he crossed to the patio door and looked out.

Pommes Frites was standing outside holding a haversack in his teeth. When he saw his master he dropped it on the path in front of him and began wagging his tail. Clearly, he was of the opinion that congratulations were in order.

Monsieur Pamplemousse soon discovered why when he undid the bag and began laying the contents out on the table.

A household fork; some lengths of line, made brown in the first instance by rubbing in soil and then by use; a piece of fine netting; the odd notched peg or two, also stained brown; a hammer; a rag soaked in aniseed; a loop of wire.

All the things considered *de rigueur* by professional poachers the world over. The fork would be used for spearing the tail of a trout and lifting it out of the water after tickling; the hammer and the pegs would be for holding the netting down; the aniseed rag would come in useful for putting any other dogs off the scent should a gamekeeper be in pursuit. The wire loop would be for snaring rabbits, or perhaps for catching hares. Taken individually, most of it was innocuous enough, but in practised hands they could become deadly weapons.

The one item Monsieur Pamplemousse would have expected to find, a knife, was missing. Because it had been used? It was an unanswerable question. But . . . something about the weight of the empty bag didn't feel right. Running his hands under a layer of canvas at the bottom he came across something even better: a Swiss 9mm SIG Model P210 revolver. As he recalled, it had been made exclusively for the German government just prior to the war, mostly for use by their Border Police. He sniffed the end of the barrel. It had been fired recently. Removing the eight-round box magazine he found there was one bullet missing.

The evening suddenly took shape again and over a late meal in his room he took stock of the situation.

It was all beginning to add up. The way the other dog had immediately run off when it heard the cry of *asseyez-vous*. Training dogs to obey reverse commands had been a favourite trick of poachers when he was a boy. He knew more than one person who had got off having pleaded not guilty to the charge of possessing an animal for the express purpose of recovering game. 'Why, when I called out for him to stop, he simply ran off! Do you call that training?' Old habits died hard.

For the second night running sleep came hard to Monsieur Pamplemousse. The contents of the bag, which he had distributed under his pillow for safekeeping, were unyielding and had a particular smell about them which kept him awake. Pommes Frites had no such problems. What with one thing and another he fell asleep almost as soon as he closed his eyes. Rhythmic snores filled the room.

Monsieur Pamplemousse woke early and after a shower, quickly dressed, collected all the bits and pieces from under his pillow and replaced them in the bag. He looked around for somewhere to hide it. It wouldn't do to have a nosy room maid come across it. In the end he decided to put it in the Twingo for the time being, but first he went to the refrigerator and removed a plate on which reposed a large black *boudin*.

His comings and goings disturbed Pommes Frites, who immediately went into the other room asking to be let out.

The sky was still clear outside, the air crisp, if smelling somewhat of fertiliser. No one could call it pleasant, yet in its way was it not somehow reassuring? A reminder that come what may and despite everything, as immutable as the fact that spring followed winter, the wheels of life had to keep turning.

Pommes Frites, on the other hand, had different priorities. He hadn't been entirely idle while he was asleep. The way he saw it was this. That his master was apt to get into trouble, often through no fault of his own, was something he knew from long experience. Some people simply happened to be accident prone and needed protecting. In Pommes Frites view it was up to him to provide such protection and to take what measures he thought necessary from time to time.

For a brief moment or two he eyed the *boudin*. Then a sense of duty took over. First things first. Lying alongside it was the vibrator. He picked that up instead. Whenever one went off it seemed to spell trouble.

So it was that for different reasons hound and master each went their separate ways. Having concealed the bag beneath the passenger seat of the Twingo, Monsieur Pamplemousse went back to his room, while Pommes Frites, his mouth suspiciously full, disappeared to begin the difficult task of finding a suitable burial site. For a few minutes all was peace.

All of which made the explosion when it came all the more terrifying because it was so totally unexpected. It would have been mind numbing at any time, but somehow it was even more so when it was barely eight o'clock in the morning. For a moment or two it felt as though the silence which followed could have been cut with a knife.

As Monsieur Pamplemousse climbed to his feet

he heard a woman scream, then the sound of shouting and the pounding of feet. Someone began knocking frantically on his door. He made his way across the room and turned the security catch. It was Shinko.

'Thank God you're all right! You *are* all right?'

Monsieur Pamplemousse felt himself all over. 'I appear to be in one piece,' he said, 'when it might well have been any number. That is sufficient to be thankful about for the time being.'

He removed a shard of glass from his jacket and looked around the room. There was glass everywhere. It was something else the architect hadn't bargained on. And who could blame him? He'd been asked to design a hotel, not a nuclear bomb shelter. If no one was injured it would be something of a miracle. Perhaps the design was right after all. His room had borne the brunt. Had the building gone upwards rather than sideways it would have been another matter. Where the Twingo had been parked there was now a gaping hole.

'How about Pommes Frites? He wasn't . . .'

Monsieur Pamplemousse shook his head. 'He wasn't in the car, if that's what you're thinking. He was doing his morning rounds. Burying something, I think.' He gave a wry smile. 'Fate plays strange tricks. My mind was occupied with other matters and I forgot to give him his Wellingtons. They were in the car.'

As he was speaking Pommes Frites appeared in the doorway. He was wearing his 'hard done by' look. Hiding evidence on his master's behalf was one thing. Inadvertently swallowing it was something else again. Not only had he swallowed it, but the force of the explosion had been such that it practically went straight through him in one go, bypassing his digestive tracts in the process.

Shinko stood back while master and hound were reunited. Words were unnecessary. In any case their moment of joy was short-lived. In a very short space of time the room became crowded with interested parties; passers-by, near neighbours, members of staff, someone who announced himself as 'the Security Officer'. . . Pommes Frites made himself scarce.

As soon as Monsieur Pamplemousse had got rid of everyone he telephoned the Director.

'I have bad news for you, *Monsieur*. The Twingo has been destroyed. Blown up.'

To Monsieur Leclercq's credit his immediate thought was not the loss of the car and the cost to himself, but for the well-being of others.

'You have escaped injury, Aristide?'

'*Oui, Monsieur.*'

'And Pommes Frites . . . ?'

'He looks a little shaken, but otherwise he is unharmed. He was out burying something when it happened.'

'Not another near tragedy involving a *boudin*, I trust?'

'I fear so, *Monsieur*. The hotel has a delicatessen in the village and I bought him a large one as a treat when we were out shopping yesterday. It was meant for his breakfast. He must have been hiding it for safe-keeping . . .' Monsieur Pamplemousse broke off in mid-sentence. The plate he had taken out of the refrigerator was in two pieces on the floor. The *boudin* lay untouched where it had landed. He looked around, but Pommes Frites had disappeared again. He was heading towards the gates and he seemed to be in a hurry.

'It's enough to put him off them for ever more,' said the Director. 'Please let me know if he needs counselling.'

'On the contrary, *Monsieur*,' said Monsieur Pamplemousse. 'I think if he finds whoever was responsible for the outrage that person will need first priority.'

'You must return to Paris at once, Aristide . . .'

'But, *Monsieur* . . .'

'That is an order, Pamplemousse. Start packing immediately. I will arrange for a car to pick you up and take you to the nearest *gare*.'

Monsieur Pamplemousse gave a shrug as he replaced the receiver. It wouldn't have happened in the old days. On the other hand, there was nothing more he could do in Pouligny. The chief was right; one way and another the whole thing had become a *débâcle*. The sooner he was out of it the better. Apart from that, it was high time he and Monsieur Leclercq had a heart-to-heart talk.

He wondered if he should search out Claude before he left, then decided against it. Some things were better left to fate.

Seeing a movement outside he noticed Inspector Lafarge rooting about in the snow and he went out to greet him.

'Look what I've found!' Lafarge held up the blackened remains of a Wellington boot. The expression on his face said it all. Triumph was writ large.

'Whoever was responsible must have returned to the scene of the crime. Probably looking for the murder weapon or some vital clue they have lost. It will be revealed when the weather clears.' He glanced around and nodded towards some tracks in the snow. 'It looks as though they panicked and started running around in circles.'

'There was nothing inside the Wellington boot?' asked Monsieur Pamplemousse innocently.

'Does it look like it?'

'Whoever had it on might not have been wearing

209

any socks,' said Monsieur Pamplemousse. 'There could be some toe prints. Not as good as fingers, but useful.'

Lafarge turned away. He appeared to be mouthing something.

Monsieur Pamplemousse held out his hand. '*Bonne chance*. I have a train to catch.'

'You ought to know better than that. First, we shall need a statement.'

Monsieur Pamplemousse sighed. For once Inspector Lafarge was right.

'If you can make it sooner rather than later.'

With a certain amount of ill grace Lafarge followed him inside, and to do him justice didn't linger over the small print. Monsieur Pamplemousse gave him his home telephone number.

Packing took longer than he'd bargained for. It was worse than having a shattered windscreen. No doubt he would come across fragments of glass in his clothing for weeks to come; reminders of his time in Pouligny. He left the room with a nagging feeling of having left something behind. Or, to be more precise, something he would have taken had it still been there. If that were the case, so be it. It would turn up sooner rather than later.

The room maid was *désolée* to see him leave. And the mess! *'Oh là là!'* The girl at the check-out was *désolée*. Everyone was *désolé*. There would, of course, be no charge for his stay; Madame Dulac had sent word.

By the time various members of staff had expressed their condolences and their hopes that he would pay them a return visit, Shinko appeared to tell him the car to take him to Roanne had arrived. She led the way outside, signalling a waiter to follow on behind with the baggage.

Pommes Frites was waiting. As ever, it was hard to tell what he was thinking. He looked slightly pained. A mixture of pain and relief?

'I saw him in the distance,' said Shinko. 'He was taking the long way round.'

'I'm sorry about the boots.'

'*Pas de problème.* There are plenty more where they came from. Better to lose a pair of Wellington boots than a guest. All the boots in the world don't replace guests.'

'How *is* business?'

She made a face accompanied by a see-saw motion of her right hand. '*Comme ci comme ça.* News travels fast these days. Already there have been cancellations. Five from America. Three from Japan.'

'What will you do?'

'Move on, perhaps. It is still the skiing season. I may fill in as a chalet girl for a while. We'll see.'

It rendered his automatic response of *l'année*

prochaine redundant. He doubted if he would ever be back anyway. Not unless he were needed as a witness.

'And you?' Shinko looked at him enquiringly.

'It is back to Paris, I am afraid.'

'Brilliant! In the meantime I should hurry. There is a problem down near the gates.' She opened the rear door of a black Citroën.

Monsieur Pamplemousse followed Pommes Frites inside.

'Thank you for all you have done.'

'*Mon plaisir. Bon voyage* as they say. Take care.'

'You too.'

He suddenly felt unwarrantably sad as the door closed behind him. People entered your life and then disappeared again. Lights came on, shone brightly for a while, then went out.

Shinko was right. As they neared the entrance gates they encountered a small posse of police armed with shovels and metal detectors. They were looking at something in the long grass. One of the *gendarmes* was unreeling a length of tape, tying it to convenient trees and shrubs, cordoning off the area.

Another *gendarme* signalled his driver to stop. It looked as though they would be the last ones out for a while. The Americans were going to be late for their lunch.

Pommes Frites peered out of the side window. He seemed surprised by what he saw.

Inspector Lafarge, who appeared to be directing operations, detached himself from the main group and came towards them.

Monsieur Pamplemousse reached for his notebook, wrote a name down on one of the pages, then tore it off and folded it in two as he climbed out of the car.

He held the note up as Lafarge drew near. 'A little suggestion for later. When you are less busy.'

'We have discovered a strange vibration,' said Lafarge briefly.

'A vibration?'

Lafarge nodded. 'It is lying beneath some *caca de chien*. We are about to conduct a controlled explosion.'

'You are blowing up some dog shit?'

Inspector Lafarge nodded uneasily. 'We cannot afford to take chances.' He kept trying to see over Monsieur Pamplemousse's shoulder. 'What is that?'

Monsieur Pamplemousse turned and caught Pommes Frites' eye. He appeared to be hanging on their every word. 'It is a dog.'

'A dog! He has been staying here or is he just passing through?' Lafarge suddenly seemed depressed, as though something had connected in the back of his mind; light at the end of a very long tunnel.

Monsieur Pamplemousse's mind was similarly hard at work. He remembered now what it was that had been missing from his room. In the event it had turned up sooner rather than later. It seemed a good moment to say farewell.

'We will be on our way. But first, a word of warning. Tell whoever has his finger on the button to stand well clear of the fan.'

CHAPTER EIGHT

It was good to be back; away from the snow and back amongst the familiar sounds and smells of Paris.

Doucette had been mildly reproving about the lack of communication, until she heard about the fate of the Twingo, then she went quiet.

Heading for the office, Monsieur Pamplemousse followed the route of the 80 *autobus* for most of the way; through the Place Clichy, where the stop/start early morning traffic allowed Pommes Frites time to exchange greetings with a nodding acquaintance who for some years had kept guard outside a men's outfitters, past the Gare St Lazare and along the rue La Boétie, parting company at the Rond Point so that he could cross the Seine by the Pont des Invalides rather than the Pont de l'Alma.

The mackerel clouds were unusually high for the

time of year, and the 2CV behaved impeccably all the way, as though sensing a touch of early spring in the air.

News of their narrow escape must have filtered through to Headquarters because even the normally taciturn Rambaud managed to summon up a smile as they passed the window of his office by the staff entrance.

The Director greeted them as though they were long-lost explorers, fussing about like an old hen.

'Aristide, my dear fellow, come in, come in. And Pommes Frites too. What will it be? An *apéritif* of some kind?' He glanced at his watch. 'Or is it too early? Don't ask me for a Suze. I daresay that's what you've been drinking while you were in the Auvergne. It's too medicinal for my taste. A glass of champagne, perhaps? I have some of your favourite Gosset. The *quatre-vingt-dix* – an excellent vintage. Please make yourself comfortable.'

While he was talking, Monsieur Leclercq crossed to his drinks cupboard and opened the door to reveal an array of bottles and glasses at the ready. The welcome could hardly have been warmer had they just returned from a particularly hazardous expedition to the darker regions of the upper Amazon.

Drinks poured, all three comfortably settled – Monsieur Pamplemousse in the visitor's chair,

Pommes Frites at his feet next to a bowl of water, and the Director for once not behind his desk, but in an armchair brought in specially for the occasion – there was a momentary lull in the proceedings.

Monsieur Leclercq was the first to break the silence. 'Tell me,' he began. 'How are things in Pouligny?'

'It is my opinion, *Monsieur*, that despite everything, the Hôtel Dulac will survive. There is too much at stake. Besides, it is too good, too professional to fail. Much knowledge has already been handed down. If it comes to pass that the summit meeting is held there, it will be an enormous fillip and perhaps spur them on to even greater efforts.'

Was it too fanciful to wonder if one day Claude might assume the mantle of her illustrious relative? Time alone would tell.

'No more recycled lettuce leaves?'

'If all I believe is correct, *Monsieur*, that will be a thing of the past, along with all the other minor problems they have been suffering.'

'And the Twingo?'

'I am afraid it is damaged beyond repair. The whole of the back was blown clean away.'

The Director gave a shudder. 'Just think, Aristide, you might have been inside it.'

'That was probably the intention. Had the device been connected to the ignition instead of to the hotel paging system, as I suspect it was, I certainly would have been.'

'I should never have forgiven myself.'

'It could have been worse . . .'

'Pommes Frites?'

Monsieur Pamplemousse nodded. 'He would almost certainly have been in the back seat. He prefers it on a long journey. Then I would never have forgiven myself.'

'But how, Aristide? And why? Most of all, why? And, of course, by whom?'

'The "how" is easy, *Monsieur*. Fertiliser, saturated in diesel fuel and packed into a confined space like a car boot, is one of the simplest forms of explosive available. It is more economical than dynamite, and needs only a simple detonator to set it off. A blasting cap would have been ideal. It was probably stolen from the local quarry. A simple modification of a pager would have turned it into a switch. Pushed into the explosive mixture along with a battery, it only needed someone to press the appropriate button at the right moment to complete the circuit.

'The plan very nearly came off. Whoever it was probably intended to lie in wait for me to get in the car. He had armed himself with a person to person controller, but he reckoned without the fact that not only is the main panel situated in reception, it is also duplicated in the restaurant area and both were capable of overriding it. The preparation of *déjeuner* is usually left to the junior staff and in the confusion someone must have pressed the wrong button by mistake in order to summon a waiter and *poof!*'

'I must go through the insurance agreement with a fine-toothed comb,' broke in the Director. 'I'm sure there will be a clause in it somewhere or other about loading the boot with fertiliser. On the other hand, farmers must do it all the time. In any case, they are bound to ask the obvious question.'

'Why did it happen?' continued Monsieur Pamplemousse. 'Someone clearly felt threatened by my presence. As for who that person was . . . I think I would rather not answer that question for the time being. At least not until I have more proof.

'But first of all, *Monsieur*, and changing the subject, let me say straight away that your secret is safe with me.'

The Director looked suitably touched. 'I knew I could rely on you, Aristide.'

'It must have been a great burden to you all these years,' ventured Monsieur Pamplemousse.

'It has, Pamplemousse, it has.' The Director gazed into his glass, saw that already it was almost empty and reached for the ice bucket on a small table beside him.

While he was occupied, Monsieur Pamplemousse sought for words to express what he wished to say.

'It is not my business, *Monsieur*, but I take it Madame Leclercq knows nothing of the affair. I ask, simply because I would not wish inadvertently to say the wrong thing should the subject ever come up.'

Monsieur Leclercq blanched at the thought.

'I have always tried to keep it from Chantal,' he said. 'I promised the Founder on my honour it would remain a secret, so, apart from your good self, and fate intervened to bring about your involvement, that is the way I trust it will remain.'

Monsieur Pamplemousse stared at him. 'Monsieur Duval knew?'

The Director nodded. 'Not straight away, of course. That was the whole tragedy. Had he known from the very beginning things would have been different. I am not saying they would necessarily have been better, who can tell? In many ways Monsieur Hippolyte Duval was not a man of the world. He led a sheltered life, particularly during his later years. He was wholly tied up in the pursuit of excellence; the excellence of what he came to think of as his calling. Towards the end there was an almost Messianic aura about him. Then again, he had always been one of nature's bachelors. It is hard to picture how he would have coped with family life.'

His mind in a whirl, Monsieur Pamplemousse listened to the Director's monologue with only half an ear. 'It is perhaps fortunate for him that the occasion never arose,' he said at last.

'Our Founder was an honourable man, Aristide,' said the Director simply. 'He was never one to shirk his obligations. In his mind Claude came to represent the child he never had; someone to whom he could have passed on the result of his life's endeavours had things been different.'

Monsieur Pamplemousse gazed up at the picture of Monsieur Hippolyte Duval, viewing it with new respect.

'To have taken on his own love child, *Monsieur*, would have been an act of great self-sacrifice, but to have taken on someone else's . . . it is hard to find words. He must have thought the world of you.'

It was the Director's turn to look puzzled. 'I'm afraid I do not follow your line of thought, Pamplemousse. What are you trying to say?'

Feeling himself entering deep waters, Monsieur Pamplemousse took a deep breath and reached for his notebook. It was time for plain speaking. What was it the writer Georges Simenon had once said? 'A drowning man doesn't worry about the purity of his strokes.'

Flipping through his notebook, he found the page he was looking for; the one containing notes he had made during his visit to the cemetery in Pouligny.

'Forgive me, *Monsieur*, but we *are* talking about the same Claude?'

Monsieur Leclercq stared at him. 'I'm afraid I still do not follow you, Aristide.'

'I mean the one who was born to Madame Danièle Dulac in 1961.'

It was the Director's turn to look confused. 'No, Pamplemousse, we are not. It goes back much further than that. We are talking about the Claude who was born to a Mademoiselle Florentine Dulac in 1939.'

'But . . .' Monsieur Pamplemousse did a rapid mental calculation, 'but, unless my information is at fault, *Monsieur* himself was not even born at that time.'

'Your information is entirely accurate, Aristide, I was not even minus one.'

'Then you are not the father of the child in question?'

During the long silence that followed Monsieur Pamplemousse's last remark, a feeling of *déjà vu* came over Pommes Frites. Sensing it was time for a nap, he closed his eyes.

'I don't know what to say, Aristide.' The Director spoke at long last.

'You did tell me about your first visit to the Auvergne on behalf of *Le Guide*,' said Monsieur

Pamplemousse defensively. 'I naturally assumed it was something that happened then. A moment of indiscretion for which you have been paying the price all these years.

'Then again, there was all the secrecy with the car. The way it had to be collected and delivered. I began putting two and two together . . .'

'Not unnaturally making *cinq*.' The Director hesitated, his eyes suspiciously moist. Then, avoiding Monsieur Pamplemousse's gaze, he took the opportunity to recharge their glasses. 'And without knowing the truth of the matter you unhesitatingly risked your life for me?'

Monsieur Pamplemousse paused before answering. The plain fact was that it had been *because* of the Director rather than for him, but he doubted if he would have behaved any differently had he known the truth. Despite all his faults there was something about Monsieur Leclercq that brought out the best in people.

He nodded. 'I can only repeat, *Monsieur*. Your secret is safe with me. What has happened is past history, a matter of record that cannot be changed.'

'There I must disagree.' The Director crossed to the window and gazed out over the Esplanade des Invalides with unseeing eyes. Clearly, his mind was far away. 'History is only what we choose to remember. Worse still, more often than not it is the interpretation others choose to make of events about which, not being present at the time, they know little or nothing about. You only have to compare the history books of France and England to have proof of that. *Les Anglaises* still believe they won the battle of Waterloo.

'Make yourself comfortable. I will tell you a story. One which I trust will give you no cause to alter your resolve to keep the matter a secret.'

Clearly bracing himself for the task in hand, Monsieur Leclercq made sure the door to his office was firmly closed, took a long draught of champagne before seating himself, then pushed the glass to one side out of reach of temptation while he marshalled his thoughts.

'Aristide,' he began, 'you are a good *homme*. It is no wonder I put so much trust in you. Do you seriously think for one moment that I am the father of Claude?'

'The present Claude, *Monsieur*?'

'Of any Claude, Pamplemousse. Past, present or future. It is not a name which would sit in harmony alongside that of Leclercq.

'I see I must tell you the story from the beginning, as told to me by our Founder on his deathbed. When you hear it you will appreciate it could not have been easy for him. You will also understand why,

224

once repeated, the sorry tale must not go beyond the four walls of this office.'

'Of course, *Monsieur*. I give you my word on that.'

'It began,' said Monsieur Leclercq, 'in 1938 when, at the age of fifty-nine, Monsieur Duval set out to explore the length and breadth of France; a mammoth task even by today's standards with all the resources we have at our disposal. *Le Guide* itself was then approaching its fortieth anniversary, and it had expanded beyond all his wildest dreams and expectations. The coming of the automobile had changed everything. During the thirties people's horizons had broadened and from being a slim volume devoted to places within cycling distance of Paris, it now embraced the whole of France. Michelin was hard on its heels; others were beginning to make their presence felt.

'On the third week of his travels Monsieur Duval reached the Auvergne and late one night arrived in Pouligny; which then, as now, boasted but two hotels; the Moderne and the Hôtel du Commerce. Both establishments were ostensibly owned by members of the same family, although once again, as is still the case today, that was in name only, for the people concerned were as different from each other as chalk and cheese. The one half of the family, talented and ambitious, the other half lazy and unreliable.

'It was this time of the year; cold and snowing hard. Tired out after his long journey and stricken with influenza, Monsieur Duval settled on the first hotel he came to, which happened to be the Commerce. Influenza was a much more serious matter before the war and fortunately he went straight to bed, otherwise we might not be where we are today.

'For almost a week it was touch and go as to whether or not he would survive. The local doctor had almost given up on him, but he was nursed back to health by the owner's wife, Madame Florentine, who, much to our Founder's consternation, later tried to take advantage of his weakened state and climb into bed with him. Fortunately, he was able to draw on his reserves as he put it and he repulsed her advances, although clearly it disturbed him rather more than he cared to admit at the time, perhaps sowing the seeds for what was to follow.

'A few mornings later, when he was almost fully recovered, he woke to find her daughter, Danièle, lying there beside him, naked as the day she was born.'

'Such things often run in families,' said Monsieur Pamplemousse reflectively. 'Especially in the Auvergne, where the winters are long and hard. And remember, it was long before the days of television. Even wireless was still in its infancy. People not

226

only shared their cat's whiskers, but other pleasures as well. I well remember my *tantine* Melanie. She and her daughter ran a small establishment in the Monts du Forez until it was closed down.'

'Be that as it may, Aristide,' broke in the Director impatiently, 'and with all due respect both to your *tantine* and her daughter, this was a different kettle of *poisson*. Can you picture the scene? Our Founder by then is on the eve of his sixtieth birthday; life in many respects has passed him by. Beside him lies this ravishing, raven-haired beauty, her urgent young body pressed against his; her pulsating limbs aching to entwine themselves around him, drawing him ever closer to her. Bliss, the like of which he had never before experienced, is his for the taking.

'Doubtless refreshed by his long rest, something snapped and all the pent-up energy he had once expended on pedalling the highways and byways of France was now devoted to the task in hand.'

'You mean . . .' Monsieur Pamplemousse sat up.

The Director mopped his brow, then gave vent to a series of whistling noises as was his wont when he was skating over thin ice. 'That is exactly what I mean, Pamplemousse. History relates that when Napoleon met the coach bringing his bride, the Archduchess Marie Louise, to the Forest of Compiègne, such was his haste to consummate their marriage he threw caution to the wind and boarded it there and then. However, I venture to suggest even the Emperor could scarcely have been more impatient to catch up on lost time than was our Founder.

'Listening to Monsieur Duval's account, I commented at the number of times they . . .' once again the Director broke into a series of whistles '. . . and he expressed surprise.

'"*Ça n'est pas normale?*" was the expression he used, Pamplemousse, and he said it with such an air of innocence I honestly believe he meant it.'

Monsieur Pamplemousse stole another quick glance at the portrait over the drinks cabinet. One never really knew other people, and that was a fact.

'Still waters run deep, *Monsieur*.'

The Director followed his gaze. 'The truth of the matter is Monsieur Hippolyte Duval had never experienced any kind of relationship before. He had always been much too busy, so he had nothing to compare it with; no benchmark as it were. From all he told me it was the first and only time such a thing ever happened to him. And as so often happens on such occasions the perfidious side of Dame Nature took its course. Nine months later, a child was born.'

'But I thought he was such a model of rectitude,' exclaimed Monsieur Pamplemousse. 'Metaphorically speaking, he must not have been wearing his cycle clips.'

The Director glanced uneasily towards the Founder's portrait. 'An unhappy choice of phrase, Pamplemousse, if I may say so. One does not always take one's cycle clips to bed with one. In any case, he had long since given up bicycling everywhere. It was the golden age of motoring. Why, in Lyon alone there were over one hundred car manufacturers. Monsieur Duval was by then driving an eight-cylinder Delage. It is no exaggeration to say that the very thought of all those pistons going inexorably up and down, propelling the great monster at speeds in excess of 100kph must in themselves have acted as a kind of aphrodisiac to the young lady sharing his moment of rapture, spurring her on to even greater efforts. It is no wonder she became pregnant.

'As for rectitude, such was our Founder's probity and devotion to duty, having said goodbye to his love, before leaving Pouligny he had *déjeuner* at the Hôtel Moderne and enjoyed it so much he awarded the restaurant one of his newly instituted Stock Pots.'

'You don't think his judgement was at all clouded at the time, *Monsieur*?'

'I think not, Pamplemousse. Rather the contrary, and in view of everything that has happened to the Hôtel Moderne over the years, I think he showed remarkable prescience.

'All the same, and in view of what later transpired,

229

the award must have acted like a red rag to a bull to the brother who ran the Hôtel du Commerce, especially since he didn't receive so much as a Bar Stool by way of recognition. It marked the start of a feud that has lasted until this very day. The two branches of the family have been at loggerheads ever since.'

'There is a saying, *Monsieur*, that the *Auvergnat* is less agile than the goat, but more hard-headed than the mule.'

'For "hard-headed" read "stubborn", Pamplemousse,' grunted the Director. 'You have no need to tell me that. The whole thing is like a Sicilian vendetta, or a Greek tragedy, depending on which way you look at it.'

Ignoring the remark, which struck him as being a bit too close to home for comfort, Monsieur Pamplemousse thought of the present day Claude. Did she fit the latter description or had she inherited some of the Founder's ambitions and strength of character? Time would tell.

'But did Monsieur Duval express no wish to marry the girl?' he asked.

'That is the tragic part of the story,' said the Director. 'He had no idea she was pregnant. He wrote to her many times, but his letters were returned unanswered and in the end he assumed that as far as the girl was concerned he was simply a ship that had passed in the night.

'He might never have known until the day he died had he not taken it into his head about a year later to pay a return visit to Pouligny, probably in the hope of re-establishing contact. And there he learnt the truth.

'It seems that by a cruel twist of fate, shortly after his first visit the owner's wife, Madame Florentine, died of influenza. She may even have caught it from Monsieur Duval himself. Then, when the daughter revealed the fact that she was expecting a child, and inevitably there comes a time when such things become hard to conceal, the storm broke.

'In those days being pregnant normally meant a hasty trip to the altar, but since she steadfastly refused to say who was responsible, she was thrown out by her father and went to live with her Aunt Alphonsine in Roanne.

'Some months later she gave birth to a boy and it was her dying wish that he should be called Claude after the father.'

'Claude was Monsieur Duval's middle name?'

'Even I did not know that until he related the story,' said the Director. 'He must have told it to her in great confidence.'

'And did I hear you say it was her dying wish, *Monsieur*?'

'I am afraid so, Aristide. Learning the truth from others in the village, Monsieur Duval made all haste to Roanne and there he learnt the very worst news of all. Danièle had died in labour. According to the aunt she called out the father's name again and again, but of course it was in vain. It was the only time he was to see his son.'

'A tragedy, *Monsieur*.'

'Indeed, Pamplemousse. The whole story is one of tragedy; tragedy heaped upon tragedy.

'Nowadays everyone would know about it of course, but attitudes were different then and in the interest of *Le Guide*, the whole thing was kept a dark secret.

'Consumed as he was with shame and remorse for the son he could never call his own, Monsieur Duval retired into his shell, resolving to look after the boy's upbringing as best he could. Then, when his own life was nearing its end, it was his dying wish that after he had gone I take charge of matters on his behalf. He made a *Testament Olographe* on his deathbed to that effect, and I in turn made a promise to carry out his wishes to the best of my ability.'

'A heavy responsibility, *Monsieur*.'

'*Alors!*' Monsieur Leclercq raised his hands to high heaven. 'It has not been easy, Pamplemousse. You know as well as I do what the laws of France are like in these matters. They are very strict. Circumventing them is far from easy. It is all laid down. Albeit, and largely owing to the deprivations of the two World Wars, there were no other claims on his estate, and since he was a frugal man, money is fortunately not a problem.

'I . . . we, all of us, owe our livelihood to him, and I owe him a particular debt of gratitude for providing me with a vocation that is dear to my heart. In some ways I suspect he saw me as a surrogate son.

'As always, there are ways, but as I say, it has not been easy, particularly as he was very specific in his requirements. It was his wish that any male descendant would be provided for until they reached the age of twenty-one, at which time they would have to fend for themselves. That was to be strictly understood. The money would remain in trust to provide for the upbringing of his son, should he have one, which, of course, he did, and so on down the line until such time as a daughter was born. Then all payments would cease.'

Monsieur Pamplemousse felt his head begin to reel as the awful truth dawned on him. 'With respect, *Monsieur*, did you say *male* descendants? Isn't that a little unfair?'

'Remember, Aristide, all this took place long before female emancipation. In those far-off days women didn't even have the vote. Remember, also, our Founder was himself from a bygone era. He had very fixed ideas on these matters.'

'In that case, *Monsieur*. There is a problem.'

The Director raised his eyebrows, 'Indeed, Pamplemousse? How so?'

'Because . . .' Monsieur Pamplemousse took a deep breath. 'Because, *Monsieur*, you are no longer dealing with a son.'

'You cannot mean this, Aristide.' Monsieur Leclercq looked at him aghast. 'Are you saying . . . the present Claude, the one who was to receive the Twingo, is of female persuasion?' Clearly he could hardly bring himself to utter the key word.

'I don't think she needed very much persuasion, *Monsieur*. She seems very happy the way things have turned out.'

'The Claude we are talking about is a girl?' Monsieur Leclercq got the word out at long last. 'This cannot be, Pamplemousse. Claude is a man's name.'

'It can also be used as a woman's name,' said Monsieur Pamplemousse. 'I have checked with Larousse. And in this case I think there was a very good reason.'

'Are you sure?'

'*Absolument, Monsieur.*'

The Director sat lost in thought for a moment or two. 'I have to admit I didn't ask for proof of the sex. It didn't for one moment occur to me to do so, but . . . You have met her?'

'*Oui, Monsieur.* On more than one occasion.'

'Do you by any chance have a photograph?'

'I do indeed. In fact, she specifically asked me to give it to you so that she could lay claim to the Twingo.' Reaching for his briefcase, Monsieur Pamplemousse found the envelope he was looking for and handed it across to the Director.

Monsieur Leclercq opened it and slowly removed the contents. He stared at the print for a moment or two.

'Pamplemousse,' he said at last, 'why has someone drawn a moustache on it? Is it some kind of prank?'

'I'm afraid I am responsible, *Monsieur*.'

'You, Pamplemousse? But, why? Such a charming picture – totally ruined. Is this another of your aberrations? Defacing photographs of young girls in your spare time? Have you nothing better to do?'

'It struck me, *Monsieur*, that the image bore a striking resemblance to your good self and I wanted to make sure.'

For once the Director seemed at a loss for words.

'I will have a word with Trigaux,' said Monsieur Pamplemousse, 'I'm sure he will have ways of removing it electronically.'

The Director thought for a moment. 'I would rather you didn't, Pamplemousse. Questions may be asked.' He held the photograph up to the light and looked at it more closely.

'Is this not the very same girl who appeared in the pictures I was sent only the other day? The ones showing you crouched over her prone body, much as you did with the Mother Superior in Boulogne.'

'*Oui, Monsieur.* That was how I found out about the hotel's paging system. I tried to explain at the time.'

'Did you really feel there was a likeness?'

'Only superficially, *Monsieur.* I think by then it was a case of half seeing what I was expecting to see. Looking at it again in the cold light of day there is perhaps more than a passing resemblance to Monsieur Duval.'

'You really think so?'

'There are the same high cheekbones. The ears are not dissimilar. In some respects ears are often the most fruitful area in which to make comparisons; they are pointers to a person's character. In recent years they have been the subject of much study.'

Monsieur Leclercq rose and crossed to the drinks cabinet. He reached for a bottle of cognac, then thought better of it and began pacing the room instead.

'All this puts me in something of a quandary, Pamplemousse,' he said. 'On the one hand there is the promise I made to Monsieur Duval – a promise to carry out the wishes of a dying man. On the other hand . . .

'Tell me, Aristide, you are a man of the world. What would you do in the circumstances?'

236

Monsieur Pamplemousse considered the matter for a moment or two before replying. 'I think I would take it gently for a while, *Monsieur*. Our Founder may have had fixed ideas, but he was also someone who wasn't afraid to move with the times. If he was able to make what must to him have been a quantum leap from a bicycle saddle to the leather upholstery of an eight-cylinder Delage, surely in time he would have embraced female emancipation too?'

'You think then, I should make an exception?'

'I believe Claude will make her own way in the world. She is young. She is attractive. She has a mind of her own and already she has elected to enter the world of *haute cuisine*, although if all I believe is correct she may well be in need of a surrogate father for a while. A Twingo would make a wonderful gift, and since she has been twice disappointed, once when it failed to materialise in Roanne, and again when it was blown up, it would be a shame to disappoint her a third time. But as for anything else, the world has become a more mercenary place and it might not be doing her a favour. I would wait and see. You could remain in the background in case of need.'

'Is there a mother?'

'My understanding is she left home soon after the girl was born and hasn't been seen since.'

'So there may not be another in the family for some while?'

'I think it is very unlikely, *Monsieur*.'

'Tell me, Aristide. You met her. What is she really like?'

'She is a nice girl.'

'But no better than she should be? I sensed that from the pictures I received over the facsimile machine.'

'Are any of us, *Monsieur*? Pictures do not always tell the truth. Some people acquire a reputation quite unfairly. True, she made me feel young for a while, and yet . . .'

'Come now, Pamplemousse, you are as young as you feel.'

'I am beginning to wonder, *Monsieur*. Having said that, I am not sure one would have trusted oneself with her in the Garden of Eden.'

'Autumn would have arrived earlier than usual, eh, Pamplemousse? Fig leaves would have been blown hither and thither. Displaced beyond recall?'

'Irretrievably, *Monsieur*.'

'So in the end the world would not have been such a different place?'

'*Non, Monsieur*. I fear not.'

'Good, I'm glad to hear it.' The Director rubbed his hands together. 'You have helped me make up my mind, Aristide. I am pleased to say there is sufficient money available to purchase a new Twingo. This time I may even drive it down myself.

Given all that has happened it would be good to inspect the Hôtel Dulac at first hand.'

'Would that be wise, *Monsieur*?'

'You think I shouldn't?'

'I think some things are best left to follow their own course. At least for the time being.'

The Director looked disappointed. 'But I thought it was all over. It was in this morning's *journaux*. They have arrested two men. It seems they were midgets . . . members of a travelling circus . . .'

'I think by now they will have been released, *Monsieur*.'

'You do?'

'The person who murdered Monsieur André Dulac is much closer to home than that. Earlier you asked me if I had any idea who did it. I *know* who did it. He is a man with hatred in his soul, a hatred handed down from generation to generation. In giving him a menial job as a kind of dogsbody because he thought blood was thicker than water, André Dulac thought he was bestowing a favour. In fact, he was only rubbing salt into the wound and in effect signing his own death warrant. Giving is often much easier than receiving.

'I think he is the kind of person who is constantly on the prowl, forever waiting and watching. A person who wouldn't hesitate to have his daughter christened Claude in order to feather his nest. Any

239

money you have sent has gone not on her upbringing, but to line the pockets of her father. Your letter about the Twingo, which came her way purely by chance, was the first she got to know about it all.

'What began as minor acts of sabotage, pinpricks as it were, escalated until they became an obsession. I doubt if the original attack on André Dulac was premeditated. It was probably nothing more to begin with than a violent row which got out of hand. Panic began to set in afterwards when he realised what he had done, and when he saw me making notes in the cemetery it took root.'

'And you think that was sufficient reason to try and kill both you and Pommes Frites?' asked the Director.

Monsieur Pamplemousse nodded, although deep down he had to admit he harboured doubts. There had to be something else as well.

'He could see his whole world collapsing and he became desperate. Added to that was the realisation that with his half-brother out of the way he could become the dominant member of the family. I strongly suspect he was already making overtures in that direction towards the bankers, who in turn were getting edgy about their loan.

'I think he is a member of the second oldest profession. In France he is known as *un braconnier*, in Germany *der Wilderer*, and in *Angleterre* a poacher. They are all one of a kind. It is bred in the bones and passed on from father to son. It is not something you learn at school. I think he is the man you caught a fleeting glimpse of on the tape. The man with the dog. André Dulac's ne'er-do-well brother.'

'But if you know all of these things, Aristide, what is the problem?'

'Knowing is one thing, *Monsieur*. Proving it is another matter. Don't forget, avoiding capture is part of a poacher's stock in trade. It is second nature. Everybody in Pouligny knows what the other Dulac does for a living; but even the police would be hard put to make it stick in a court of law.'

Given the undoubted complications of the Director's 'arrangements', it wouldn't be possible to get him on a charge of embezzlement either. He was literally sitting pretty.

'Pommes Frites brought me a bag. Where he got it from I do not know, but it was covered in moss as though it had been hidden in some undergrowth. It was an important item of evidence.'

'Was? You mean you no longer have it?'

'Unfortunately, no. It was in the back of the Twingo. The bag and its contents were blown to smithereens. No doubt bits and pieces will begin to show themselves when the snow melts. There was a gun – that should still be intact, wherever it is. In the meantime I have suggested to Inspector Lafarge that he pays a visit to the Hôtel du Commerce. For

241

what it is worth, he may find duplicates of the knife he has in his possession, although again, that in itself will prove nothing.

'There is a wealth of circumstantial evidence. The knife . . . the gun . . . motive . . . opportunity. Knowing about the bag Pommes Frites brought me is one thing, proving its ownership is something else again.'

'But you have seen the tape, Aristide. Was there nothing more on it apart from Pommes Frites' disgraceful behaviour? I seem to recall brief glimpses . . . while I was speaking to you on the phone. And when we played it through for the second time.'

'The tape?' It was Monsieur Pamplemousse's turn to look puzzled. 'I'm afraid I do not understand, *Monsieur*. All I saw were the live pictures as they happened.' He felt tempted to say that he only saw half of those because certain people telephoned him halfway through.

The Director looked uneasy. 'I have to admit, Aristide, that I was perhaps somewhat precipitate in telephoning you when I did, but once Pommes Frites disappeared over the horizon everybody lost interest and began talking amongst themselves. Fortunately we were recording it for posterity.

'Then, after dinner, when the ladies had gone off to do whatever it is ladies do after they have partaken of a good meal, the rest of us were lingering over cognac and cigars and Monsieur le Ministre expressed interest in certain technical aspects of the filming. He wanted to see it all over again. I promised to let him have a copy, but he couldn't wait, so I gave him the remote controller while I telephoned Trigaux issuing instructions to produce a duplicate as soon as possible.

'My mind was focused on other things, and in any case after the repeat of Pommes Frites' escapade it was hard to hear what was going on for the general hubbub. Cries of *encore!* and *bravo!* echoed round the room, but as I recall, before Monsieur le Ministre rewound the tape for yet another viewing there was a sequence where the man made a second appearance.'

Monsieur Leclercq made his way across the room and opened a cupboard door next to the drinks cabinet. It was the first time Monsieur Pamplemousse had seen inside it. The Director certainly did himself proud when it came to new equipment. It looked like a state-of-the art recording studio in miniature.

'I have the original here. I can show it to you now, if you like . . .'

'If you would, *Monsieur.*'

Pressure on a button caused a panel to slide back, revealing a slimline television screen. Returning to his seat the Director fast-forwarded through the earlier part of the tape. The sound of digitally enhanced heavy breathing woke Pommes Frites and he gazed at his speeded up performance with interest, not to say a certain amount of pride in a job well done.

For his part, Monsieur Pamplemousse was riveted by the scenes after Pommes Frites detached himself from the object of his desires. The Director was right. Following the chase over the brow of a hill, there was a momentary pause as the camera panned wildly to and fro. 'Hosepiping' as it was known in the trade. A bush swam into view, then filled the screen. The branches parted as the camera moved slowly forward. Moments later a man came into view and began concealing something down a rabbit hole. He paused, clearly looking over his shoulder to make sure he wasn't being watched. For a second or two it was as though he were being held in a still frame, then the camera panned down to reveal what he was in the act of hiding.

Monsieur Pamplemousse had difficulty in concealing his excitement. It was all there. It couldn't have been better if it had been directed by Alfred Hitchcock; or Chabrol, perhaps. Claude Chabrol at his best.

'Thank goodness I didn't wipe the tape at the time,' said Monsieur Leclercq. 'In deference to the sensibilities of the ladies I very nearly did. Fortunately, Monsieur le Ministre intervened just as my finger was on the button.'

'You said Trigaux will be making a copy, *Monsieur*?'

'Indeed.'

'We must get another off to Pouligny as soon as possible. There is no time to be lost. May I use your telephone?'

'Of course. Two *Auvergnats* coming up against one another must be worse than Greek meeting Greek,' mused the Director, while Monsieur Pamplemousse was waiting to get through.

'In this case,' said Monsieur Pamplemousse, 'to give credit where credit is due, one of them did have the benefit of a bloodhound at his disposal. It was a great advantage.'

Monsieur Leclercq reached for a button on his desk. 'The whole thing is a cause for celebration. I will get Véronique to order Pommes Frites some *boudin noir* from Coesnon. You did say the *campagne* is his favourite?'

'I did, *Monsieur*.'

Pommes Frites pricked up his ears as he heard several key words in quick succession.

'He must have been remarkably well concealed when he took the pictures,' said the Director. 'It is quite extraordinary.'

'Extraordinary sums it up,' said Monsieur Pamplemousse. He gazed down at Pommes Frites. 'He has a sixth sense in these matters. It is second nature to him, and all in the course of a day's work. Although I suspect he didn't go entirely unnoticed, which is why the attempt on our lives was made.'

'Do you think the earlier part of the tape was a calculated "diversion" on his part?' asked Monsieur Leclercq. 'That look on his face which we, the viewers, took to be undisguised gloating could, in fact, have been one of distaste?'

'Pigs might fly,' thought Monsieur Pamplemousse. 'We shall never know, *Monsieur*,' he said simply. 'Let us just say we all have our methods. Perhaps it is best left at that.'

'You are absolutely right, Aristide,' said the Director. 'There is an unhappy tendency in this day and age to destroy the reputations of those who are unable to defend themselves. Lesser mortals appear to derive some kind of satisfaction from it.'

While he was waiting for Inspector Lafarge to answer, Monsieur Pamplemousse glanced up at the portrait of the Founder. It was strange to think that all the events of the past few days were the result of one man's moment of weakness, but somehow he found it strangely warming. Paradoxically seeds must have been sown in more ways than one by Monsieur Hippolyte Duval when he visited Pouligny all those years ago.

'I agree with everything you say, *Monsieur*,' he said. 'On the other hand, it is good to know that our Founder was human after all. It will make our work that much more rewarding in future to know that at heart he was one of us.'

Read on for an extract from
Monsieur Pamplemousse on Vacation,
the next book in Michael Bond's
Pamplemousse and Pommes Frites series . . .

*Monsieur Pamplemousse
on Vacation*

MICHAEL BOND

CHAPTER ONE

'Statistically,' said Madame Pamplemousse, 'there can't be many people who travel all the way from Paris to the Côte d'Azur, only to end up being forced to watch a class of mixed infants give a performance of *West Side Story*.'

Monsieur Pamplemousse looked gloomily around the school hall. Statistically, as far as he could judge, they were the only ones; certainly there was no one he recognised from the train journey down.

'These things happen, Couscous,' he said.

'They do to you,' said Madame Pamplemousse, with a sigh. 'They don't to other people. Other people would be having their dinner by now.'

Doucette was quite right, of course, and there was no point in arguing. He only had himself to blame for waxing lyrical about the Hôtel au Soleil d'Or, and how lucky they were to be staying there on the Antibes peninsula at someone else's expense. In particular, he had lavished so much praise on the joy of sitting on the hotel's world famous terrace of an evening, sipping an *apéritif* while studying the menu as the sun slowly disappeared over the western horizon, anything less had to be an anticlimax.

And less was what they had ended up with. His employer, Monsieur Henri Leclercq, Director of *Le Guide*, France's oldest gastronomic bible, had seen to that. For the time being at least, it was a case of grin and bear it.

Glancing down at the mimeographed sheet of paper they had been given before the start of the show, Monsieur Pamplemousse's heart sank still further. According to a note at the bottom it wasn't due to end for another two hours. Admittedly that included a fifteen-minute interval, but from the way things were going they would be lucky if they saw the sun rise again the following morning. He decided not to mention it. At least the music was upbeat.

The twenty strong orchestra, made up mostly of girls from the senior school, was specially augmented in the percussion section by pupils from the junior forms manning triangles and tambourines.

'It's nice that everyone has a chance to take part,' said Doucette reluctantly.

Monsieur Pamplemousse gazed at his wife.

Speaking for himself, he had a sneaking suspicion that some of the smaller ones had only got the job because they had failed their auditions for any other kind of work, including that of scene shifting.

Who would be a teacher?

To be fair, the fact that so far the singing had failed to match up to his LP of the original cast recording was hardly surprising. Ill-equipped as they were for 'finger snapping', the Jets' arrival on the scene during the opening routine set the tone for much that was to follow. The number describing the delights awaiting newly arrived immigrants to America only came near to meriting the phrase 'show-stopping' when one of the more enthusiastic of the minuscule dancers overshot his mark and narrowly missed colliding with a Shark who was waiting in the wings to make an entrance.

Given the speed at which he was travelling, the fact that he failed to pass straight through the bass drum as he took a header into the orchestra was little short of a miracle.

Buddy Rich in his heyday would have been hard put to equal the cacophony of sound which rose, first from the percussion section, then from the main body of the orchestra.

For a moment or two chaos reigned. Tears cascaded down the cheeks of the infant in charge of the triangle as it was wrested from her tiny grasp. The harpist, her eyes closed in musical ecstasy, spent several seconds plucking the empty air before realising that her instrument was lying on its side, while the shrieks and squeals which rose from the string section rivalled that of the Sabine women as they met their fate.

At least there were no broken bones, but what Leonard Bernstein would have said about it all was best left to the imagination.

'Do we have to stay, Aristide?' whispered Doucette.

'Only until the interval,' hissed Monsieur Pamplemousse.

'Pommes Frites will be wondering what has happened to us.'

'I am sure he has better things to do,' replied Monsieur Pamplemousse. 'Besides, we can hardly invite him in. He would find it very hard not to take sides. I hate to think what might happen to some of the Sharks.'

'All the same,' Madame Pamplemousse wasn't going down without a fight, 'I really don't see why we have to meet this man – this so called "art dealer" – here of all places instead of in his gallery. *If* he has a gallery.'

Monsieur Pamplemousse allowed himself a sigh. 'My dear Couscous, we mustn't look a gift horse in the mouth. You should know by now that if there are two solutions to a problem, one of which is simple and the other complicated, Monsieur Leclercq always goes for the second. It is as inevitable as the fact that night follows day. That is the way his mind works and there is no changing it.'

'Even when it is totally unnecessary, since we plan to visit Nice while we are here anyway?' persisted Doucette.

'Especially when it is totally unnecessary. He would not be happy otherwise.'

Having delivered himself of the homily, Monsieur Pamplemousse rearranged himself as best he could on a seat which would have been barely adequate for one of the cast, let alone anyone of above average bulk.

Despite his words, he couldn't help feeling uneasy. Had he been asked to write about the many missions he had carried out on the Director's behalf since he first began working for *Le Guide*, it would have run to several volumes. Indexing them, trying to find explanations as to when and how various events seemingly unrelated to each other became inextricably entwined, would be something else again. Footnotes would abound. Cross references would have demanded yet another volume to themselves.

Their present situation was a case in point.

It had all begun with an evening spent with Monsieur and Madame Leclercq at their home near Versailles.

From time to time the Director and his wife took it into their heads to invite those who worked in the field, the Inspectors – who were, after all, the backbone of *Le Guide*'s whole operation – to dine with them. It was a form of bonding: almost the direct opposite of the American habit of allowing junior staff the privilege of wearing casual clothes to the office on a Friday, since it was a case of dressing up rather than dressing down.

That apart, given the surroundings – the beautifully tonsured lawns, the immaculate gardens, not to mention the food and the wine – few would have wished to forgo the pleasure. Only the wives had reservations, for in their case it inevitably meant an extra visit to the hairdresser on the day and as the moment drew near long heart-searching over what to wear.

It was after dinner, when Madame Leclercq and Doucette had retired to another part of the house to talk about whatever it was ladies talked about on such occasions, that Monsieur Leclercq first broached the subject of a holiday in the South of France.

As soon as Monsieur Pamplemousse saw the bottle of Roullet *Très Rare Hors d'Age* cognac appear he knew something special was afoot. However, by then he was overflowing with the good things of life and in a benevolent mood; his critical faculties on hold for the time being, his guard lowered.

The Director chose the moment of pouring, when he had his back to Monsieur Pamplemousse, to strike.

'Is everything well with you, Aristide?' he asked casually. 'It may be my imagination or perhaps even a trick of the light, but it struck me earlier on this evening that you were not your usual self.'

Monsieur Pamplemousse, who until that moment had been feeling particularly at peace with the world, suffered a temporary relapse. He took a grip of himself. Two could play at that game.

'It has been a busy twelve months, *Monsieur,* what with one thing and another.

'There was the time I spent on the Canal de Bourgogne and the unfortunate business with your wife's aunt. Admittedly her brother was in a sense once removed, having lived for most of his life in America . . . Well, given the fact that he was shot, I suppose you could say that in the end he was twice removed . . . but as things turned out it was scarcely a holiday . . .'

'Ah, yes.' The Director made haste to pass one of the large Riedel balloon-shaped glasses; filled, Monsieur Pamplemousse noticed, with rather more

7

of the amber liquid than he would have wished given all that had gone before. The Director wasn't one to stint his guests. Meursault with the *goujons* of sole, Château Cos d'Estournel with the pigeon and cheese, Barsac with the peaches and cream. He would have to watch his driving on the way home.

'Then,' he continued remorselessly, 'there was the time earlier in the year when you had me pick up a car in Paris – the Renault Twingo you were giving to the illegitimate granddaughter of our late lamented Founder – and drive it down to the Auvergne. Again, if you remember, a home-made bomb planted in the boot wrecked my hotel room and very nearly took me with it . . . Hardly what one might call all in a day's work.'

The Director seized on the mention of Monsieur Hippolyte Duval, founder of *Le Guide*, to raise his glass in silent homage and effectively cut short Monsieur Pamplemousse's soliloquy.

Cupping it in his hands to warm the contents, he inhaled the vapour it gave off, then gave a deep sigh. 'Aaah! It is no wonder they call it "the angel's share".

'I know I have yet to thank you properly for all you did in both instances,' he continued, 'and on previous occasions too; but mention of them gives me the opportunity to make amends. All work and no play makes Jacques a dull boy and I think the

8

moment has come when you should both indulge yourselves by investing in some quality time.'

The use of the Americanism confirmed Monsieur Pamplemousse's suspicions that the Director had being paying yet another visit to the New World; he usually returned armed with a supply of the latest expressions. He also noted the sudden use of the plural tense.

'My car is overdue for its first 300,000 km service,' he said dubiously. 'Since Citroën stopped making the *Deux Chevaux*, parts are often hard to come by. Doucette and I have been thinking of taking the train to Le Touquet and spending a few days with a distant cousin of hers.'

Monsieur Leclercq emitted a series of clucking noises, as though experiencing a momentary seizure. 'I was picturing somewhere rather more exotic, Pamplemousse. Somewhere further south; on the shores of the Mediterranean, *par exemple*. A spell in the sun will do you both the world of good.'

'Le Touquet can be very invigorating in June,' said Monsieur Pamplemousse, 'particularly when the wind is from the north-east, but if you get down to the beach early in the morning and find a suitable sand dune to shelter behind, there are the sand yachts to watch . . . provided *les Allemandes* haven't got there first . . . just lately Doucette has been suffering with her back . . .'

'In that case,' said the Director, 'a week sitting on the beach in Le Touquet will probably do her more harm than good.'

'I have been studying Shiatsu recently,' persisted Monsieur Pamplemousse. 'It is an ancient Japanese art where you apply pressure with your thumbs to various parts of the body . . .'

'If you do that kind of thing behind the dunes, Pamplemousse,' said Monsieur Leclercq severely, 'you may find yourself in trouble with the beach patrols.'

Draining his glass with a flourish to show that to all intents and purposes the matter was no longer up for discussion, his voice softened. 'Neither Chantal nor I will take "no" for an answer, Aristide. I will have my secretary book three seats to Nice on the TGV – *Première Classe* – no doubt Pommes Frites will wish to accompany you both.

'It is our way of saying "*merci beaucoup*". Please do not deprive us of the pleasure.' Normally Monsieur Pamplemousse would have bided his time, waiting for some kind of catch to emerge. It always made him feel uneasy when the Director addressed him by his first name. But despite everything, the words had been spoken with such simplicity, such innocence, humility even – a quality he rarely associated with the Director – he found himself wavering.

'If that is what you really wish, *Monsieur . . .*'

'It is, Aristide. It is. And I know Chantal will be especially pleased.'

And on that note the evening had come to an end.

They were barely out of the front drive and heading for home when Doucette broke the news. 'Isn't it wonderful, Aristide? Madame Leclercq has been telling me all about it. And really, all they want in return is that we should pick up a piece of artwork for them. Apparently it is too precious to be entrusted to a carrier. All the same, it seems so little in return for so much. Mind you, knowing the Director I'm sure it won't all come out of his own pocket.'

Monsieur Pamplemousse resisted the temptation to say he would be surprised if any of it did, but Doucette had been so excited at the thought of an unexpected holiday he hadn't the heart to throw cold water on it. Anyway the die had been cast and the whole thing sounded innocent enough.

So what was new? Wasn't that the way most of his adventures on the Director's behalf had started?

For the same reason it came as no great surprise when at the last minute the arrangements had been changed; picking up the painting or whatever it was at the concert rather than from the gallery itself.

As order was at last restored and the orchestra took their places and began tuning up again he glanced around the hall. Apart from the seating, it

11

really was the most luxuriously equipped school he had ever come across.

'Not like it was in our day, Aristide,' whispered Doucette, reading his thoughts.

Monsieur Pamplemousse couldn't help thinking it wasn't like it had been in anyone's day.

As for the technical equipment . . . On the way in they had passed a state-of-the-art sound mixing console, the sole purpose of which seemed to be that of achieving a balance between the orchestra and the individual soloists, all of whom were equipped with concealed radio microphones. Video cameras were dotted around, set to record every moment of the production. According to the programme, edited tapes of the complete show would be available at a future date. As for the lighting rig: apart from the footlights, there were spots and fillers galore over the stage area. Suspended from bars which could be raised and lowered by remote control from somewhere behind the scenes, they wouldn't have looked out of place in a television studio. He wondered where all the money had come from.

What was it the hotel concierge had said? 'It is the only mixed infants school in France with an eighteen-hole golf course.' It had sounded like a local joke at the time.

It seemed that everyone, apart from the builders, had profited from the largesse bestowed on it by some unknown Russian benefactors. The contractors had been screwed into the ground, and in the end had gone bankrupt along with the architect, having had to pay out a vast sum for failing to meet the completion date. Rumour had it that almost immediately afterwards the same company had set up under another name further along the coast constructing a vast multi-storey car park, but not before having been suitably recompensed for their previous loss.

It struck Monsieur Pamplemousse there might have been more to the story, but a party of Americans had come along wanting to know where the action was of an evening and caginess had set in, so he had been unable to pursue the subject.

He resolved to claim the rest of his hundred francs worth of information later.

He stole a glance at the programme. It couldn't be long before the interval. The scene had already changed to a bridal shop and Maria's first solo number.

If he had been asked to single out a possible contender for future non-stardom, he would have opted for the infant who had been chosen for the part. Her rendering of the song 'I Feel Pretty' was a triumph of imagination over reality. The only mercy was that she made no attempt to play the large musical instrument she had round her neck.

Monsieur Pamplemousse couldn't help reflecting that her father must have made a sizeable contribution to the school's facilities; a science lab, perhaps, or a new gymnasium at the very least: perhaps even the air-conditioned hall itself.

'I don't remember there being a balalaika in the original version, do you Aristide?' whispered Doucette.

Monsieur Pamplemousse shook his head as he looked up the child's name on his sheet: 'Olga Mugorvski'. It sounded like a disease.

Joining in the dutiful applause at the end of her number, he fell to wondering why it was that different nationalities were often so instantly recognisable. Without even knowing the child's name he would have put her down as being Russian, or at least of Baltic extraction. It was the same with the Americans and the British; Italians and Germans too. It wasn't simply a matter of features; the cheekbones, the shape of the nose or the mouth, or even the way people dressed. It had to do with many things: their bearing for a start; the way they looked at you; the way their hair grew, and even more importantly, the way it was cut. With some there was a whole history writ large. There was the openness of people from the American Midwest; with Russians it was possible to detect a lifetime of suffering in the lined faces of the old.

The young mistress who was directing the orchestra was a case in point. Dark, slender and vivacious; she couldn't possibly have been anything but French. She would have made a wonderful Maria. There was a virginal quality about her snow-white *doudounes*. During a spirited rendering of 'Gee, Officer Krupke!' they threatened to burst forth each time she lifted her arms in order to signal various musical high points. It was safe to say that not a father in the audience remained unmoved. Hopes having been raised along with the arms, breaths were held, but to no avail.

Rapturous applause greeted the end of the number and cries of *encore* filled the hall. When the lights came up to signal the interval and it became clear that many a dream would remain unfulfilled, those nearest the back made a beeline for the ticket desk to put their names down for the video.

'Wonderful, weren't they?' whispered Doucette.

'Heavenly,' agreed Monsieur Pamplemousse. 'Round and firm, yet not lacking movement when the moment was ripe, as in the final crescendo.'

'Aristide! I was referring to the children.'

Monsieur Pamplemousse stared at his wife. Truly, however many years two people spent together, there were moments when communication remained at a very primitive level. And if that

15

were the case when discussing a matching pair of innocent *doudounes* – which possibly, although perhaps in this day and age not necessarily, remained as yet untouched by any human hand other than her own – what hope was there for the rest of mankind? Heads of State conferring over such complicated matters as the disposal of nuclear weapons would have their work cut out.

'*And* she wasn't wearing a brassiere.' Clearly, as far as Doucette was concerned that was the end of the matter. Her copybook had been irredeemably blotted.

Monsieur Pamplemousse knew better than to argue. In any case the general hubbub as those around them stood up to stretch their legs put an end to further conversation.

Leading the way to the back of the hall, he hovered near the entrance, half expecting to receive a tap on the shoulder, or at the very least catch sight of someone carrying a large parcel, but he looked in vain.

'Perhaps he is waiting for us in the hotel,' said Doucette, as the minutes ticked by.

Monsieur Pamplemousse gave a grunt as they turned to go back inside. 'That's not what the concierge told me. The message was very specific. Besides, he would have given us the tickets if . . .' He broke off at the approach of a small figure, a tray rather than a balalaika suspended from its neck.

'*Pragráma. Souvenir Programsk.*' You could have cut the accent with a knife.

Seen from close to, the child looked even more unprepossessing than she had on stage. Not so much a mixed infant as a mixed-up one. He wondered what she would become when she grew up. A tram driver, perhaps? Or a crane operator? If it were the former he wouldn't fancy the chances of anyone running for the last one back to the depot late at night.

Ignoring a bowl filled with large denomination notes held in place by a paperweight, he took one of the programmes and felt for some small change.

'*Nyet!*' The child shook its head and held up four pudgy fingers and a thumb. '*Cinq cent francs.* Fife hundreds of francs. Eet is for good cause. Eet is in aid of school library.'

Monsieur Pamplemousse froze, then slowly withdrew his hand from a trouser pocket.

'*Nyet pour vous aussi!*' he said, with feeling.

'Aristide!' Doucette looked shocked. 'She is only small.'

'She may be small,' said Monsieur Pamplemousse, 'but I am not in the market for purchasing a deluxe edition of the complete works of Alexandre Dumas.'

He could feel the child's eyes boring into him as she made her way round the room and joined a small group standing at the far side of the lobby. He guessed it must be her parents: the woman, *très solide*, with tightly permed hair, was how he imagined the daughter would be in thirty years' time. As for the father, he was definitely one of the old guard; short, barrel-chested, far removed from the current breed of slim, Armani-clad Westernised executives. Apart from the open-necked shirt and gold chain, he could have passed for a Nikita Khrushchev lookalike. The top of his shaven skull looked like an old warhead from an Exocet missile, and was probably twice as dangerous. Better a face to face meeting than have it trained on him while his back was turned.

Following a brief conversation, they all turned. The girl pointed towards Monsieur Pamplemousse. The father nodded, then patted her head affectionately before sending her on her way. None of which would have worried him overmuch if she hadn't made a throat-cutting gesture with her free hand as she left. It caused hearty laughter all round. Her father passed a comment to another man, who responded with a smile that was rendered even more mechanical by what appeared to be a row of steel teeth. In all, it could only have lasted a half a minute or so, but he was left with the distinct feeling that he hadn't heard the last of the matter. He hoped the daughter didn't have a birthday coming up.

'I didn't like the first one's ears,' said Doucette, reading his thoughts.

'And I don't like tiny tots who go around demanding money with menaces,' growled Monsieur Pamplemousse. Nor, he might have added, did he like ones that smelt strongly of pot, but then she wasn't the only one. Looking around he decided he might just as well be in Leningrad or Vladivostok. He felt an alien in his own country.

'You can tell a lot from ears,' said Doucette darkly. 'That man's are much too small. They look as though they were stuck on as an afterthought.'

It was true. Since he had left the force, ears had become the subject of a great deal of scientific study. Prints taken from windows and doors often yielded as much, or more, information than fingerprints. On the other hand, he wouldn't want to try taking the Russian's ear-prints with an inkpad.

'Shall we go?' asked Doucette, as the audience began drifting back to their seats. 'It doesn't look as though he's coming, and I really can't stand much more.'

'If that is what you would like, Couscous,' said Monsieur Pamplemousse, hoping she wouldn't choose to argue the point.

Outside, it was like walking into an oven; much as it had been when they stepped off the train that afternoon. The air was heavy with the sensuous smell of mimosa and bougainvillaea. Pommes Frites came bounding out from behind an ancient olive tree, pleased to see them as ever. If he was surprised to find them leaving when everyone else was going in the opposite direction he showed no sign, rather the reverse. Monsieur Pamplemousse registered the fact that his brows were knitted, and his eyes, or what little could be seen of them beneath large folds of flesh, looked slightly glazed; sure signs that he had been thinking. Of what, would only be revealed in the fullness of time, if then.

In truth, had he been taxed on the point, Pommes Frites would have had to admit he wasn't too sure himself, although a brain scan might well have revealed an unusual number of local disturbances in the overall pattern of his thought processes. In fact there were so many undercurrents darting hither and thither he might well have been asked to make a further appointment, for it was really a matter of sorting them into some kind of logical order.

His master's prophecy on the way down that there would be new smells for him to smell and new trails for him to follow had proved all too true, although in the end both had come to an abrupt end in the car park. Putting two and two together had led him to one inescapable conclusion. The person responsible had gone off in a car OR – and this was where confusion began to set in – had been *driven* off. And if that were the case, then it must have been in the boot rather than at the wheel.

It was for such powers of reasoning that Pommes Frites had been awarded the Pierre Armand Golden Bone Trophy for being Sniffer Dog of the Year in the days when he, too, had been a member of the Paris *Sûreté*.

'It was a funny evening, didn't you think?' said Doucette. 'I don't want to keep on about it, but I still can't understand why we were supposed to meet up at a school concert instead of in Nice.'

'Ours is not to reason why,' said Monsieur Pamplemousse. He watched as Pommes Frites disappeared into a clump of pine trees in order to investigate the sound of cicadas in a deserted *boules* area, the sodium lights casting a ghostly shadow as he dashed back and forth sniffing the ground. 'I'm sure he had his reasons. Perhaps he didn't want us to go to his shop.'

'In that case, why didn't he turn up?' said Doucette. 'Seeing all those Russians makes me wonder. I'll say one thing for them. They all had lovely shoes. You could see your face in them. It reminded me of the time I gave your new slippers to the Victims of Chernobyl Disaster Fund. You were cross with me because you said it would be a miracle if they ever got that far. You said they were probably already being worn by some fat member of the Russian Mafiya toasting his feet in front of a roaring fire in his *dacha*.'

21

'It is not quite the same thing, Couscous,' said Monsieur Pamplemousse mildly.

'We don't even know how big a painting it is,' said Doucette. 'Perhaps that's why Monsieur Leclercq wanted us to go by train. Have you thought of that?'

Monsieur Pamplemousse had to admit the answer was 'no'. Trust a woman to home in on details.

Beyond the pine trees they passed a row of shops he didn't remember being there the last time he had visited the area: a couple of boutiques, a photographic shop and another with drawn blinds.

Pommes Frites caught up with them as they drew near the hotel, then ran on ahead and pushed his way through the revolving door.

The concierge was nowhere to be seen and his number two rushed out from behind the counter as an errant tail made furious contact with an ancient dinner gong positioned near the lift. Other staff materialised within moments. An elderly women, her hair in curlers, appeared on the stairs.

'It used to be the fire alarm, *Monsieur*,' said the man reprovingly.

Monsieur Pamplemousse reached for his wallet. 'It is good to know it still works,' he said cheerfully. 'So often these things are mere token gestures. I must congratulate the management on keeping it as a standby. You never know when it may come in useful.'

Returning to his station the man reached for their room key. 'The young *Monsieur* is staying here?' he asked. 'Because, if so . . .'

'He has his own inflatable kennel,' said Monsieur Pamplemousse. 'I have made the necessary arrangements with the beach attendant. I will take him down there in a moment.'

'I will see that a bowl of water is made available for him before he retires for the night, *Monsieur*. Still or sparkling?'

'Still, *s'il vous plaît*,' said Monsieur Pamplemousse. 'Evian.'

Having made a note, the deputy concierge preceded them to the lift, opened the doors, stood back to allow Pommes Frites entry after his master and mistress, then pressed a button for the third floor.

'It's a wonder he didn't ask what *journal* he likes in the morning,' said Doucette, as the doors slid shut. 'Or *journaux*.'

'He will go far,' said Monsieur Pamplemousse. 'Good hotel concierges are worth their weight in gold. Their importance cannot be overestimated. For the regular visitor they provide a sense of continuity; of timelessness in an ever-changing world. For those in search of information they have no equal. I must make a note.'

'More work,' sighed Doucette. 'I thought this was meant to be a holiday.'

'When it comes to hotels and restaurants,' said Monsieur Pamplemousse, as the lift came to a halt and the doors slid open, 'there is no such thing as a holiday. The Director will still expect a report. Besides, I have a new laptop to test. It is one of the latest models – on the cutting edge of computer design.'

'I would have expected nothing less from Monsieur Leclercq,' said Doucette.

Monsieur Pamplemousse wondered if he detected a note of irony in her voice, but she was already gazing at her reflection in the dressing table mirror. Women always had so many things to do before performing even the simplest of tasks, like going downstairs to dinner.

His colleague Bernard was fond of saying that his wife even applied fresh make-up before ringing up the butchers to make a complaint.

The terrace was crowded when they arrived back downstairs. All the prime tables nearest the sea had either been taken or had a reserved notice on them, and they were seated in a corner near the bar.

'It is more romantic,' whispered the female sommelier by way of consolation as she lit a candle for them. Any complaints Monsieur Pamplemousse might have harboured melted away.

Pommes Frites curled up under the table, his head resting between his two front paws, looking as though his mind was millions of kilometres away on another planet.

Dressed in the clothes he had worn to the concert, Monsieur Pamplemousse felt lost without the notebook he normally kept hidden in a pocket of his right trouser leg. Reduced to relying on his memory, he fell silent while he concentrated on the food. Doucette seemed to catch the mood too and, tired after their long journey, they retired to their room as soon as the meal was over, foregoing their usual *café* in case it kept them awake.

Before he went to bed, Monsieur Pamplemousse took one last look over the balcony at the scene below. The hum of conversation was a polyglot mixture of French, German, English, Japanese, plus a sprinkling of American voices.

In the distance he could see the twinkling lights of the coast road. An aeroplane drifting low overhead lost height and its landing lights came on as it headed towards Nice airport. Over it all the sound of a piano drifted up from the bar; recalling the days of Scott Fitzgerald and Zelda, whose photographs still graced the walls. He wondered whether it merited an ear plug – *Le Guide*'s symbol for background music, and decided not. From the medley of tunes he picked out Noel Coward's 'Room With a View' and Cole Porter's 'Night and Day'. There was a selection of Maurice Chevalier hits. It was really very pleasant.

In the time it had taken them to come up in the lift more people had arrived. Their own table had been cleared and reset, and one of the larger reserved tables overlooking the sea was now occupied by the Russian group he had encountered at the school. Seen from on high with the moonlight shining on it, the father's head looked more like a tiny *Anglais* Millennium Dome than a warhead.

He wondered what mysteries it might contain and if the family were just passing through or staying in the hotel. Probably the latter, since there was no sign of the daughter. Very likely she was sitting up in bed stuffing herself with whatever Russian children stuffed themselves with when they played 'midnight feasts'. In her case it would be a packet of something pretty solid; dried sturgeon on a stick perhaps, with a large bowl of vodka-flavoured ice cream to follow. With luck it might make her sick.

The sommelier materialised with a bottle and presented it to the father, who nodded his approval, as well he might. Even from two floors up Monsieur Pamplemousse recognised the distinctive label with its host of brightly coloured bubbles.

It was a Côte Rotie La Turque from Guigal. Tasting dispensed with, the girl disappeared, returning a few minutes later with a second bottle. At anything up to 2000 francs a go, they were certainly pushing the boat out. The concierge was right about where all the money came from in that part of the world.

'Are the people who were at the table behind ours still there?' called Doucette.

Monsieur Pamplemousse leant precariously over the edge of the balustrade. Once again there was the ubiquitous smell of bougainvillaea. 'I think not . . .'

'There were three of them – an American and another couple. The American caught my eye because he reminded me of Tino Valentino. Remember . . . he was singing at the dance you took me to at the *Mairie* last Christmas. He was much shorter than I expected.'

'Those sort of people often are,' said Monsieur Pamplemousse, his mind on other things. 'Remember Tino Rossi?'

'The woman was definitely English, or I suppose she may have been Scottish – she had that sort of skin. She reminded me a bit of that American film star we used to go and see years ago – Greer Garson. I'm not sure what nationality her husband was. He kept looking at you. Once or twice I thought he was going to come across.'

'You should have said.' It was the story of his life. Where Doucette was concerned the action was always behind him.

'I had a feeling it might mean more work for you and we are here on holiday. I think he may have been English too. He knew enough to raise his thumb when he was ordering. Not like so many foreigners who use their forefinger and then wonder why they get two of everything. But then at the end of the meal he left his fork with the tines pointing upwards. It was the kind of mistake that must have happened a lot in wartime. It's the little things that give you away.'

'You would have made a very good detective, Couscous,' said Monsieur Pamplemousse.

'Do you really think so?' Doucette sounded pleased as she turned off her bedside light. She gave a yawn. 'I haven't lived with you all these years for nothing.'

Monsieur Pamplemousse was about to turn back into the room when his attention was caught by a movement at the far end of a long jetty to the right of the hotel.

A fishing boat had appeared out of the inky blackness of the bay and was tying up at the end of the jetty. It rocked violently as two shadowy figures struggled to land their catch. He smiled to himself as he caught sight of Pommes Frites hurrying towards it to see what was going on. He wished he had his energy.

'Would you like me to lower the shutters, Couscous?' he called.

But in the words of the famous Scottish poet, Sir

Walter Scott, 'Answer came there none.' Doucette was already fast asleep.

It wasn't long before Monsieur Pamplemousse was in the same blissfully happy state. His last waking memory was that of hearing a series of three distant howls. Long, drawn-out and mournful, they were reminiscent of the wailing of a North American train crossing the prairie at night. Or so it always seemed to be in Westerns.

Had he been in a slightly less comatose state, he would undoubtedly have recognised it for what it was: the plaintive cry of a frustrated bloodhound making his way homeward to an inflatable kennel.

Though the first was man-made, and the other reflected nature in the raw, they both performed a similar function.

As Pommes Frites settled himself down for the night, he had the satisfaction of knowing that while he might not have brought his master running, at least as far as those on the terrace of the Hôtel au Soleil d'Or were concerned, they couldn't say they hadn't been warned.

If you enjoyed
Monsieur Pamplemousse on Probation,
read on to find out about other books
by Michael Bond . . .

∽

To discover more great fiction and to
place an order visit our website at
www.allisonandbusby.com
or call us on
020 7580 1080

MONSIEUR PAMPLEMOUSSE
AFLOAT

When the Director of *Le Guide* offers up a holiday on the
Canal de Bourgogne, Monsieur Pamplemousse is unaware
that there are strings attached – several, in fact. Things
are not quite as peaceful as they seem among the vineyards
of Burgundy, and family rivalries and resentments from
long past culminate in a series of strange occurrences.

Monsieur Pamplemousse, accompanied of course by his
faithful bloodhound Pommes Frites, finds himself caught up
in the trouble. Before the holiday is over the crime-solving
duo will have to cope with the perils of portholes, a dead
parrot, missing undergarments, the advances of a Marilyn
Monroe lookalike, and an assassin disguised as a nun . . .

MONSIEUR PAMPLEMOUSSE
ON VACATION

Monsieur Pamplemousse is looking forward to a well-earned break in the South of France courtesy of his employer – all he has to do is collect a piece of artwork for *Le Guide*'s Director. But when his contact fails to show and a dismembered body is washed up outside the hotel, the holiday mood evaporates.

As Pamplemousse struggles with the case (and with modern technology) his ever-faithful bloodhound Pommes Frites is on hand offering proof why, during his time with the Paris *Sûreté*, he was one of their top sniffer dogs.

MONSIEUR PAMPLEMOUSSE
HITS THE HEADLINES

When Monsieur Pamplemousse is offered a free ticket to Cuisine de Chavignol, France's premier TV cookery programme, he is unenthusiastic – there's something fishy about the culinary expertise of its host. But when the show ends in disaster, Pamplemousse finds himself with something more suspicious on his hands: a puzzling case of murder.

Soon Pamplemousse and his faithful bloodhound Pommes Frites find themselves caught up in a bizarre world of illusions, unrequited lust and blackmail in high places.

MONSIEUR PAMPLEMOUSSE
AND THE MILITANT MIDWIVES

It isn't every day that a coffin explodes during a funeral ceremony. Barely escaping with his life, thanks to a warning howl from his faithful bloodhound Pommes Frites, Monsieur Pamplemousse can only wonder who was behind the explosion . . . and if they were also responsible for the demise of the coffin's inhabitant.

But then another urgent matter comes to his attention: a terrorist group is planning to poison the food chain. Monsieur Pamplemousse, together with Pommes Frites and a rather strange ally, must spearhead an elite group to stop the catastrophe . . .

MONSIEUR PAMPLEMOUSSE
AND THE FRENCH SOLUTION

When Monsieur Pamplemousse gets an urgent summons from the Director of *Le Guide*, he knows that there is trouble at the top. But neither he nor his faithful sniffer dog, Pommes Frites, expects the trouble to involve a nun who is in the habit of joining the Mile High Club or a full-scale smear campaign targeting *Le Guide*'s credibility.

Someone has been spreading worrying rumours among the staff and infiltrating the company files – awarding hotel prizes for bedbugs and praising egg and chips signature dishes. Even Pommes Frites has become a victim of the assault. It could all spell the ruin for *Le Guide*, but Pamplemousse is on the case . . .